The Return of Mary Blu

The Return of Mary Blu

A SEQUEL TO BIG BUSINESS

GERRY HUERTH

LitPrime Solutions
21250 Hawthorne Blvd
Suite 500, Torrance, CA 90503
www.litprime.com
Phone: 1-800-981-9893

Published by LitPrime Solutions: 10/27/2023

ISBN: 979-8-88703-311-2(sc)
ISBN: 979-8-88703-312-9(e)

Library of Congress Control Number: 2023920233

Contents

Chapter 1

When Mary Blu finally made her move, she had very little left: an old, flabby sofa, some mismatched silver ware; a couple of pans with scorched bottoms, a few chipped ceramic plates, a set of once clear plastic glasses now made hazy by years of handling, and a large cardboard box stuffed with old clothes from the now defunct Blu household. In her flight, Mary had left behind what she could and took what she needed, except for that box. And a big box it was, stuffed with layer upon layer of clothes carefully packed by her mother in the course of a lifetime in that house on the dead end street. Mary had thrown a last and less tidy layer onto that box as she, the final resident of that house, fled the past.

That first day of her exile, she did meet that strange little girl with the dirty hair and pink Barrette…what was her name? She was shaking her head in a repetition of confusion…Roxanne, that's it. With so much banging and so many things ending, her memory seemed fuzzy.

She glanced over at the yellow scarf that she had draped over an edge of the sofa and stopped shaking her head.

She determined to anchor herself in the dark walls of her tiny apartment on Franklin Ave, a few doors down from the liquor store. There she attempted to hold at bay police sirens that screeched all around her and unshaven men sullenly waiting for who knows what on the nearby corner. She would sit for hours whispering the word "now" to herself; her big, blank face attempting to light itself with curiosity. But she found the present a flimsy, unsteady place. As soon as she would whisper "now" and steady herself long enough to look out the window, "now" would slip out from underneath her feet leaving her once again sinking into the depths of a past she struggled to forget.

Some mornings she spent hours awake in bed, eyes pinched closed, struggling to keep the slippery day out. Mary Blu was very determined. But even in that vacuum which she tried to create around herself, some vague presence kept nudging her until exasperated, her big body would begin stirring, creaking the springs of the bed. She'd sit up to start the morning. Although during each day that followed, she would surreptitiously peak into darkened corners and cabinets just to make sure she was alone. Still not satisfied she would lug out that big box from the closet, just to make sure that nothing or nobody was hiding behind it.

Every day her whole body would strain and huff as she pulled on that big box in a tug of war. Even though it was the final and most ambiguous addition to her possessions, it certainly was the most trouble. Even worse, its unexamined contents kept attempting to entice her curiosity.

Mary, in fact the whole Blu household, had done their best to avoid curiosity and anything else that could lead to mischance. Any sort of discovery was greeted with anxious silence. Certainly in Mary's current, unfortunate state, anything smelling of mystery was to be avoided. From the start that box reeked of possibilities, and possibilities all somehow turned into heart pumping confusion.

Two weeks ago, she stumbled upon the box in the attic; Mary had a way of stumbling into things. She wasn't exactly saying goodbye to her home; that would have seemed to final. She was simply wondering through the contents of that old house before they would be abandoned to the past. Even though it was a warm summer day and the attic was hot enough to roast a chicken, Mary paused by the box. Though she didn't dare examine the contents, she noticed the word "SAVE" carefully printed out on the cardboard box in her dead mother's very own script. Mary studied that word as if it were some mysterious hieroglyph and then obediently wrestled the box down the attic stairs and added it to the meager pile of possessions that she was taking with her.

In fact even when her family had crowded that house, no one knew of the existence of the box except of course for her mother. True, Mary did notice that periodically things would disappear from her closet and drawers, old things that she didn't want to wear anymore let alone think about, like her first pair of gym shorts. Occasionally her father would complain that a favorite, raggedy shirt was missing. Even her sister Arlene's old poems would occasionally seem to vanish into thin air; although things had a way of disappearing around Arlene. At any rate none of the family seemed to really notice the vanishings. Not that anyone in that household seemed to want to look too closely at anything let alone remember. No one even thought to ask that timid wife and mother why she spent hours every Sunday evening up in the attic.

Right before Sam the Junk Man came to take away the contents of that house, Mary topped off that already bulging cardboard box with one last layer of things: her mother's favorite dress, one of Arlene's paper bags full of feathers, and Mary's nursing uniform.

Mary dragged everything to the sidewalk. She sat sweating on the old sofa waiting for Sam and a tomorrow she couldn't imagine. When he finally arrived she didn't know whether she was relieved or terrified. On that steamy Saturday morning they piled the last remaining cntents of the house into the old truck of his that used to transport pigs to the slaughter. As a kindness he even packed up Mary and making his hurried stop at Franklin Ave.

There by the curb of that busy street, she stumbled out of the truck and pulled down several paper bags and the very large box, but her movement into the future was finally hung up trying to angle the sofa off. Sam looked down from the height of his cab as Mary strained with the bulky sofa. Sweat, salty as tears, dripped down her tangled hair onto her face. Finally Sam shoved his door open and with a little grunt stepped down from his eminence. As a parting generosity he helped her pull the sofa up to her new home. Mary was left to maneuver the big box which kept erupting its contents as she dragged it up the stairs.

In fact even when the box was placed carefully in the center of the room some force inside it seemed to keep erupting, spilling out clothes. First she tried stuffing that box in the closet of her bedroom. The first morning of what was to be a new life, when she was pulling that box out to look behind it, she found a pair of her mother's gloves resting mysteriously on the very top of the heaped box.

That night she thought she heard stirring in the closet and on that second morning she found a black sleeve of her father's good suite draped over the cardboard edge. After the next particularly noisy night in the closet, she found her first training bra looped over a corner of the box; that was the last straw. She lugged that box out of the closet next to the bed in hopes that her vigilance would prevent it from acting up.

That night when she got up in the dark to go to the bathroom, she stumbled over the box leaving half the contents spilled out and sprawling next to her. Perhaps the bedroom was the wrong place for it.

She tried moving it into the kitchen where its restless mass wouldn't disturb her sleep or trip her up. But that evening after she turned her back on the box to place a TV dinner in the oven, she noticed Arlene's first communion veil draped over the entire box. Mary who had a predilection for spilling things was so anxious about the snowy white headdress that she tripped over a rickety chair that some former tenant had abandoned, and was sent tumbling, turkey, gravy, potatoes and shriveled peas onto the kitchen floor. The kitchen would not do for such purity. After all she remembered how Arlene looked that morning long ago, like a little virgin bride.

Finally Mary pulled that restless box into the living room next to a window that looked out on Franklin Ave. The box seemed a little more peaceful there; not that it remained completely quiescent. Why last evening while Mary ate her supper in the kitchen, one of her white nursing caps worked its way to the edge and after balancing on the cardboard rim toppled on to the floor.

It seemed no matter how quietly Mary lived, that box kept brewing surprises which she would resolutely and blindly stuff back into the bulging cardboard. She was such a large person in such a small apartment, and under the best of circumstances wouldn't have had room for that heap. And this wasn't the best of circumstances, not by any means, even without the box's unruliness. Still, that box dogged her attention. She would spend hours blankly staring at its mass thinking nothing in particular. Once in a while she stared at it long enough so that her eyes almost by accident climbed over the top and peeked out the window onto the busy life of Franklin Ave.

Yes it really wasn't so bad after all, except in late afternoons when the sky dimmed and her apartment filled with shadows. She would sit on that sofa peaking over the box at the smudges on the window as she slowly became drenched in darkness, wondering how all her caution had come to this.

Not that Mary was particularly introspective. She

hovered mutely somewhere between feeling and expression. But still a voice eked through her apprehension: how had she come to this? She had been so careful.

The question rang through her, and while she studied the smudges on the window above the box, a paper worked its way to the top of the heap and something fluttered down to the floor. She pulled her ponderous weight out of the sagging depths of the sofa and was just about to blindly stuff it back into the oblivion of the box when she noticed by the spooky glow of twilight outside her window that it was a page of notes that she took at that first meeting with Rita Reinke and Hernando when all three, bright eyed made plans to set up their business, The Rainbow.

She stood in that moment between day and night holding that piece of paper, eyes pinched closed, shaking her head. How could anything be fool proofed from her bumbling self? One partner absconded with the funds and the other went on a blood curdling manic vendetta. Who would have thought that this pot lay at the end of The Rainbow?

Those last days in the business, Mary was like a maiden in a city whose carefully constructed walls had been breached by horse men from the steppes; the ominous was no longer vague…it was streaming into the breach. Silently she waited within those broken walls for the inevitable. Screams didn't matter anymore as she peaked out to see the first blood soaked man who approached her with a sword and a teeth-bared smile. That's when the whole city began shrieking, not for mercy…that was out of the question; but simply in naked terror. And then pain ripped through her.

Mary's hand automatically crunched up that paper and stuffed it deeper into the box. She fled back to the sofa where she made herself breathe deeply, all the while wiggling her toes like Ariadne had taught her, until her descent into the past was cushioned. She settled once again into this darkened room where she set to staring at the box in hopes of quieting it. Yes, it really wasn't so bad, after all, the frantic velocity of falling finished, in this dominion of a tiny apartment. She sat, eyes unfocussed, a large, middle aged woman peeking out at that inevitable destination on which she had landed.

Then her gaze once again would begin crawling up to those smudges on the window. That's when the very first lights in the evening beyond the glass prickled her eyes. She shifted her buttocks on the lumpy cushion; those lights kept staring back at her sometimes even blinking, letting her know that indeed it was at she to whom they were looking. They even seemed to beckon to her like some insistent even annoying companion, pleading with her to look beyond the smudge of self-preoccupation. Those lights surprised her long enough for her to actually peer through the glass, her whole body shuddering in a sigh of apprehension. But that sparkling distance didn't hurt her; perhaps it only wanted her attention. She nodded her head in the gloom.

On that shore of the evening, at approximately 8 p.m. she was born again, perhaps reluctantly, but born enough to stand up in the darkness of the living room and turn the lights on.

That's when she heard the soft harmonica music coming out of the night. After all things really weren't so bad, the music sifting through the slim gap of partially open window, sighing so sad and sympathetic that she wanted to cry. She was emboldened to begin her preparations for supper.

Walking into the narrow kitchen, she grabbed a package of instant macaroni and cheese from one of the cupboards that hemmed her in. She stuck her thumb through an end of that box and with a sense of magnificent accomplishment, pulled off the cardboard top.

Then that large innocent face of hers, waiting like unmolded clay for form, noticed the rectangular block of broccoli already resting like an island in a pan of water on the stove. That was a remnant of her first attempt to make supper, before the box had interrupted her. Not that she liked to eat green things, except perhaps for that lime green jello salad with canned pear halves that her mother used to make.

Just that morning Mary had been reading MADEMOISELLE. Every year her sister Arlene had signed up for the Publishers Clearing House Sweepstakes, and every year she, blind child of hope, felt certain that she would win. Well, one lonely morning, before Mary fled her home and just after Arlene left for Alaska, the Publishers Clearing House Sweepstakes contest form slipped into the her mail box; Mary missing her sister, filled out that intricate form. With some tentative sense of accomplishment, she decided that it was only fair that she order a magazine, especially since she couldn't rule out the possibility that she might actually be the lucky person to win millions of dollars. Besides she had never subscribed to a magazine before.

For one whole day she studied the folded pages covered with postage stamp sized magazine covers. She finally tore out the stamp on which was an innocent, girlish face that was reminiscent of a younger Arlene. With just a tad of embarrassment Mary licked its backside and placed it on her entry form. Then in preparation for her ambiguous future she wrote the address where she would soon be moving.

Even though the millions of dollars passed her by, yesterday MADEMOISELLE arrived at her apartment, with page upon page of fresh feminine faces, some secret to happiness lurking behind their smiles. Even better, there were page upon page of articles sharing those important secrets...how to apply the right makeup, how to flatten your tummy, how to dress, how to diet, but most important how to have that special, perky MADEMOISELLE attitude that lets the world know that you are young and beautiful; too bad everyone else isn't.

That very day, Mary had read an article called "Hollywood Tips on Beauty and Health, or Ten Days to a Younger More Glamorous You." She learned that eating broccoli would make her skin soft and dewy like a tulip; hence the source of the green rectangle in the pan.

Tip number two was even more exciting and daring: a little glass of red wine would not only bring some color to her doughy face, but also protect her heart. Mary knew she needed all the help she could get to safeguard that vulnerable organ of hers so prone to breaking.

While the harmonica music from somewhere wafted through the summer night, Mary set a single place for herself at the table, another orphan abandoned by the previous tenant. Then she scooped a gooey, yellow mass of macaroni and cheese out of the pan and plopped it onto her plate. Overcoming her reluctance to green, she placed two spears of broccoli on her plate. Finally she unscrewed the top of the cheapest wine she could find. She had been so relieved that the nice man in the liquor story had put it in a paper bag that almost made that suspicious bottle look like a carton of milk. Now she poured the bright, red liquid into one of those plastic glasses that her father had once received for filling his car up with gas. After glancing out the window to see if anybody was watching, she lowered her bulk onto the chair.

She inhabited that yellow, second story window, her large jawed face balancing on her delicate neck. Then she stared out tentatively curious about the sparkling night.

A siren started screeching. That delicate neck of hers wilted as she slumped down into her chair in vain hope of not being noticed. The screeching slowly faded into the night leaving the faint residue of harmonica music. After a minute huddled in her chair, the bulk of her body began to stir, as if some resolve were rising from the heap of herself. She sat up straight, almost formidable, and with her right hand picked up the glass with deep red fluid in it, smelled it for a moment, then tipped it to her mouth. The redness touched her lips. Her face prickled with surprise as the taste of red, the sad music, and the night coalesced into something like contentment.

With the redness warming her face in waves of reassurance, she explored that night outside her window and for a moment wondered if somewhere behind one of those points of light resided a person like her, looking out from a window into the darkness.

Her face trembled and opened like some pale, night blooming flower; then intently she bent over her supper and began eating.

When the music outside finally stopped, she nodded at her empty plate, stood up and cleared the table. She walked over to the sink, turned the hot water on, and maybe it was the wine, she cavalierly aimed a plastic bottle of dish detergent towards the splashing water, and before she knew it, the sink was crowned with an impressive pile of suds.

When she finished rinsing the suds off the final dish: the daring glass that held the red wine; a troubled look tightened her face, as if some frightening necessity perched at the horizon of the sink...yes, tomorrow she needed to look for a job.

Chapter 2

Griffin was wary of his toes. Even at their most relaxed, they pointed down digging into the ground as if waiting to set his short, hairy legs into motion. He didn't want to even think about his toe nails, they curved downward like sharp, horny hooves. Not that he let many people view those extremities unadorned; although once, in fact for years, he spent whole shoeless summers in Georgia splashing in puddles and prancing up clouds of red mud.

That was before he began living in a world of contingencies, or was it simply that he began wearing shoes? Besides he was a small man, not Napoleonic, not cute, simply small. In fact so small that he kept slipping through any wedding engagement that happened to snare him. Or maybe that too was the fault of his toes; even human shod, inside they pranced, clawing through the most careful plan.

All dressed up in his security guard uniform and a

slightly apologetic smile, there was barely an indication of those toes restless for freedom. But if you looked closely you could see his eyes, wild and excited, poke out through the camouflage of his ordinary life, as if he were playing a faint melody that waited for some resonant response.

In fact to most people the only indication of that restless yearning was those plaintive melodies he played on the harmonica each evening as another day slipped away into darkness. As his hands warmed the battered harmonica, memories and hopes rippled through his body. His cheeks would begin gently puffing, lips puckering, whispering in strange communion with that warming object as the melodies of his heart reached out to the night. He would smile secretly under that head of hair that even at fifty kept sprouting coarse and thick; a few strands even crowding down his forehead poking out just above the bridge of his nose. Needless to say, he always played with his shoes off.

Not only had he pranced through any marital opportunities, but he also kept slipping through jobs. In fact the whole idea of a career seemed like an ambush. He worked as a janitor or a nursing assistant; but most often as a security guard...unless he needed to carry a gun. For all his unshod wildness, anything that carried a premeditated threat troubled him. The mere thought set his toes to wild drumming. Playing the harmonica came soft and easy, so soft and easy that he didn't even expect any thanks for turning the city on each evening.

That very night, after he finished playing in the now dark old apartment of his, he laid his warm moist instrument carefully in the cradle of a folded red bandana. His face intent, listening for the echoes of his melody; he shed his clothes and slipped into his unmade bed that smelled of ginger and sweat.

He slept for two hours.

At ten p.m., he woke in the darkness, sat up, and once again suspicious of his toes, pulled on his black socks. Walking to his dim closet, he stepped into his regulation, blue security guard uniform. For the briefest of moments he switched on the light. Glancing at himself in the mirror that hung on his bedroom door, he lifted both arms, placed his hands on his forehead, and with somber determination flattened his stubborn hair into a facsimile of submission. Then he positioned his security guard hat on his more docile head.

He set out to do his duty at a warehouse cross town that held fruit from all over the world. He especially loved the smell of oranges, although he liked the smell of almost everything...pungent, sour, sweet, even rotten, all those odors penetrated his black regulation shoes, and set his toes in motion. That night, after a solitary trip across town, he stepped off the bus into a deserted industrial park. Instead of trees, dark, blank-eyed, brick buildings towered around him. He walked two blocks to a shadowy building on which "International Fruits" had been printed in now pealing letters barely visible even in daylight. He pulled out a huge ring of keys. They jangled like lonely chimes as he opened the door. He flashed on the lights and raced over to press in the security code before sirens would be set off screeching through the night.

For the next eight hours, he walked up and down the stairs and into each room, marching sentry as the smell of different kinds of fruit wafted through him, curling his toes. He almost lost control of those extremities as he passed through a room full of ripe pineapples. Whenever he began becoming drowsy that night, he simply had to walk through that pineapple room to be jolted awake with pleasure.

At 7 a.m., he walked out of that warehouse imprisoning the tropics, and stepped out into morning. People were marching into the brick buildings, shoulders hunched, heads and necks thrust forward as if they were pressing through a blizzard, even in late August.

His toes frustrated in their confinement steered toward home and freedom.

He stepped onto a crowded bus that drenched him in the smells of cologne, sweat, toothpaste, and cigarettes; he sat down next to a tidy, slim man in a perfectly pressed suite. Twitching his nose Griffin knew that his carefully groomed companion had forgotten to brush his teeth. Not that Griffin minded; he just knew it.

Chapter 3

At the corner of Nicollet and Franklin, Griffin stepped out into the morning, but before his toes could actually frolic in the privacy of his apartment, he stopped at Surely's Diner, home of the $1.99 breakfast, coffee not included. Even half a block away, he could smell fried bacon and coffee strong enough to curl anybody's toes. He stepped faster towards his destination, not just into a restaurant, but into a state of mind.

The front door of Surely's was propped open in a futile attempt to catch a breeze or any stray coolness that could replace the hot smell of grease and the crackle of frying eggs. Inside the clientele sat silently engulfed in a haze, hardly able to exchange a word in the last overblown luxury of summer.

Anybody who wanted a fast cup of coffee served with a smile, went somewhere else. The denizens of Surely's had a flexible perhaps even a resigned approach to time. For them etiquette consisted of not dropping cigarette ash in someone else's coffee. The owner, Shirley D'Allesandrini set the tone. She could fix that $1.99 special consisting of 2 eggs scrambled, hash browns fried to the consistency of a brillo pad, and two pieces of white toast with some butter like substance smeared on them; all before she exhaled her cigarette. Shirley like fate, didn't believe in choices.

Inside, seated at one of the black Formica topped tables, Tex mopped her beefy face with a red plaid handkerchief. Turning her head to the person sitting to her left, she said "Yup" with a kind of cosmic acceptance and took another gulp of her black, steaming coffee. She was a large cowboy-booted woman from Cleveland with hair cut so short it buzzed. Her plate, carefully mopped by toast, stood as a testament to her determination to live even this lazy day to its fullest.

The object of her wisdom, sitting to her left, was Dannie, a delicate looking Nlack Man with a shiny wig sitting on his head like a bird ready to take flight. When Tex turned to him, Dannie nodded and then with his right hand reassured the black bird nesting on his head. Dannie, actually Mr. Dannie Spain to his customers was a hair dresser. Like Griffin he was also from Georgia, but had lived on the other side of a racial divide where no shoes was just a state of being. For Dannie, a turquoise silk shirt, tight pants of some synthetic fiber that glistened in the light, and black leather shoes so shiny that he could blind people on a sunny day, were symbols of defiant accomplishment.

This particular morning in late August was one of those mornings that followed a night that never got around to cooling. People walked through air so wet and warm that their steps squished against sidewalks that were already being stoked by the morning sun...a rare occasion in Minnesota when people actually forget the winter and for an ill considered moment wish for cold.

Dannie Spain wasn't faring as well Tex in the hot heavy air of Surely's. The black shiny locks of his wig, once carefully oiled back, kept falling limply down his forehead and over his eyes. He looked at Tex. "Honey, I just don't know what to do with this hair. I guess it's the price I pay for beauty."

Tex uttered "Yup" as another damp curl drooped over Dannie's face.

His valor recognized, Dannie stared patiently at his pancakes that were soaking up the imitation maple syrup on which margarine floated like an oil slick. They were both waiting for their companion.

Tex saw Griffin first. She could see that he was in his element, a squishy, humid day of smells and dreams. His porcupine hair freed of the regulation hat stuck out defiantly in all directions. He skittered down the sidewalk between sluggish people who dreamed about forgetting their jobs to find a cool place in the shade in which to lie naked...free at last.

Griffin dove out of that sluggish stream and into Surely's door, eyes, bright beads, and hair, stiff bristles holding drops of moisture at their ends. He shook his head and whole body down to his toes, not so much to rid himself of wetness, but for the shear pleasure of twisting and squeezing that damp morning.

While one solitary drop of sweat slid down Tex's nose, she said "Yup" with a flickering smile and once again picked up her cup of coffee. Her two friends were finally corralled.

Griffin's head darted around the restaurant and settled on his two waiting companions. "Pineapples, ripe pineapples last night. When I die just stick a bunch of ripe pineapples in my coffin and let me be."

Dannie looked up from his pancakes. "Honey, who wound you up this morning? Don't you know that this is a bad hair day, so bad that at this very moment people are crowding emergency rooms with fatally wounded egos. If people weren't so busy rushing to work, they'd see each other and run away screaming."

The shiny beads of Griffin's eyes squinted for a second as he pulled up a chair. "You look all fresh and dewy this morning, Mr. Dannie. Those bangs of your make you look mysterious. They're down right alluring."

Tex who was carefully watching her companions through the steam rising from her coffee cup said, "Yup."

Suddenly all three started laughing as if that sluggish sour morning had cracked open to a kernel of fun. Somewhere in that laughter Griffin found the $1.99 special placed in front of him by the faster than light hand of Shirley, the dowager queen and cook of Surely's.

For the next half hour, despite the vicissitudes of weather and fortune, the three sat quietly in each other's company without making contingency plans, like fruit ripening on a lazy summer day.

Just about when Dannie had finally given up on the

whole idea of pancakes and was looking up at the clock above the lunch counter right next to the black board that advertised chipped beef for $2.25, he noticed a large woman, dressed in a pale green skirt with a shiny white blouse buttoned right up to her chin walking past the window outside. As she faltered across the sidewalk, he wondered if by any chance she had stuck her finger in an electric socket recently. Her hair stood on end in muddy blond chaos. Not that Dannie generally noticed women.

It wasn't just her hair. Something about the way her large head stuck out anxiously in front of her hesitant shapeless body, that made Dannie want to place his hand on her shoulder and stop her long enough so that she could fall back into some semblance of harmony. Only after that would he say, "Honey you've got to do something about that hair of yours."

By this time, Dannie's unrelenting focus had caught the attention of Griffin and Tex. All three watched the figure slyly peeking into the cafe window as if she didn't want anybody to notice that she was looking. Now she was going past the open door. Her head kept thrusting forward resolutely, her body stuttered, balking at some enticing and terrifying possibility. She moved in a funny syncopation, her torso stalling while her head attempted to maintain the forward momentum. Then she passed out of their sight.

As Tex took another sip of coffee, she looked to her companions. "Seems like a lot of work for such a piss hot morning."

Griffin nodded at the economical wisdom of his

friend. "She must be new to the neighborhood." Just then he noticed his toes curling in his shoes. "She sure is a big, old gal."

Dannie, a connoisseur of incongruities, was just about to say, "Honey, now there's a lady with a story."

But even before "honey" had passed his lips, that disconnected form reappeared in view walking backwards. Her body had finally taken charge and was pulling that unwilling head towards the door of the cafe. Even Shirley looked up from the sizzling griddle and released a curious puff of cigarette smoke. At the open door the backward momentum of the large woman halted. After a moment of paralysis, that form turned forward and allowed her bobbing head to take precedence again...Mary Blu walked into the cafe trying not to see if people were looking at her. She half stumbled over a chair; her whole form jangling in embarrassment. Like some ship at sea caught in storm, her body heaved forward desperately making its way to the safe harbor of the lunch counter where she could slide up to the round cushioned stool and settle precariously on the eminence of her dry dock.

While most the denizens of Surely's were watching Mary's procession, she kept whispering to herself that nobody was looking at her. In fact to distract herself from her unreasonable embarrassment, she placed the newspaper that she had just purchased from a funny metal box outside, on the counter and studied it as if her entire life depended on its contents, not that she was interested in the news, weather, human interest, entertainment, or even the funnies. She had a desperately more important destination...the employment section. She shot a head bobbing, timid little glance out into to the restaurant, just to prove to herself that no one was looking. She saw two beady, bright eyes topped with porcupine hair fixed on her, and buried her head back in the newspaper with a furious crumbling sound.

Just as her eyes were focusing in on the fine print of the employment ads, Shirley smashed her cigarette into the counter, straightened the red ribbon in her hair, executed a dramatic spin, and rushed over to Mary. "Hey doll, what cha want?"

At one time Shirley had been a hoofer in New York City, until she discovered her true calling and returned to the place of her birth and opened up Surely's cafe. She still hummed show tunes and chewed gum between cigarettes.

Mary's eyes peaked from side to side, wondering who the doll was, her head adamantly refusing to look up.

"Hey you with your face in the paper. Cat got your tongue or something? Ya, you over there with your blouse buttoned up to your ears."

Mary's face went hot, and she finally succeeded in jerking her head up to see a very thin woman with blood red lipstick and black hair dramatically shot through with a vein of green.

"Well doll, what cha want, I don't got all day...I gotta living to make."

The restaurant was spinning around Mary, and at its very focal point around which everything orbited, was a pair of hands, one sinewy hand holding a stub of a pencil cocked for action and the other hand holding a grease smudged tablet. Mary knew that she was supposed to say something. "Well, ah, I haven't eaten out much. My mother used to say that there's no excuse for having someone cook your breakfast when you can do it yourself. But you see I'm looking for a job today and decided that maybe just this once...besides I usually just have a bowl of cereal." Mary noticed the hand holding the pencil began to twitch. "Um, Do you maybe have some cereal and a glass of milk? I mean only if you have it."

Shirley laid down the tablet and pencil and lit another cigarette. She took a long drag all the while starring at her newest customer. Finally she exhaled into Mary's face. "You gotta be kidding!"

"Oh I wouldn't kid you; that wouldn't be nice of me, but if you think I should order something else..."

Shirley took another deep drag and dutifully, after all she was a professional, jotted down the order muttering, "Takes all kinds." She darted back into the counter.

Mary again directed her attention to the safety of the newspaper, after all she had to do a very important task this morning. Her meager savings were running out.

She just had to find a job soon, and she didn't want to go back to nursing. Her whole nursing career had been a series of blunders culminating in that last horrible calamity. She simply wanted to live a life where her clumsy person wouldn't always be making mistakes and hurting someone. That's not so much to ask...is it? With that determination under her belt, she actually started to become a little curious about the place that she had stumbled into...a real cafe.

She poked her head up to the right; so far all clear. A man in a dirty tee shirt was grumbling to himself as he sipped his coffee and filled in the blanks of a crossword puzzle. Now she poked her head up and to the left. Her face exploded in terror. Three pairs of eyes were staring at her. Yes they were definitely fixed on her. Her head jerked down so fast that she almost fell off the stool. She swallowed nervously and buried herself so far down into the newspaper, that she could have wrapped her head in it.

She fell into a fox hole of absolute confusion and lost track of time and space in the endless rapid fire memory of all her past blunders.

A hand stuck out of chaos and pressed softly but insistently at her left elbow.

She couldn't bury her head any deeper into the newspaper and opening her eyes finally surrendered to that hand.

A voice spoke from the general direction of the small hairy hand. "My friends here and I were wondering if you'd like to sit at our table...seeing it's by the window. Looks like you need a little more light to read the newspaper. You wouldn't have to look so closely."

Mary couldn't raise her head out of the newspaper, but managed to turn her head and open her eyes in the direction of that intruding voice. She found herself staring straight into a face with small, shiny eyes nestled under thick coarse hair. A few of those hairs were poking out of his forehead and pointing at her. The man was so short that he barely had to bend to catch those frightened eyes of Mary.

Her whole body wobbled unsteadily as she turned her face back into the newspaper. From the other side, Shirley sprang at her with a glass of milk and a large bowl of corn flakes.

"Hey doll, watch out. I don't have casualty insurance, and the way you're spinning around, you'll knock somebody over."

The intruding male voice from behind her began speaking again. "Shirley, why don't you place that stuff over on our table. She needs more light to look at the paper. You don't want her to go cross eyed do you?"

Mary heard hissing coming from Shirley's general direction followed by the sound of a dress swishing impatiently from behind the counter. "Well, follow me doll."

Mary lumbered up to a standing position, head still hunched over, eyes peeking from side to side. The short, hairy man guided her halting form from the rear.

With the resignation of a sheep headed to the slaughter, Mary followed Shirley. Mary kept trying to straighten her incongruously delicate drooping neck. Her mouth opened. "My name is Mary, um, Mary Blu." She wasn't looking at anyone, but seemed to be simply announcing her presence to the world.

Heads popped up in surprise all over the restaurant at the sound of such a tiny voice coming from so large a body. Tex, a woman of few words and many concerns, stepped up and out of her chair, took off an imaginary hat and said, "Mighty pleased to meet you Mam. In case you haven't figured it out, this fine lady here is the one and only Shirley of Surely's Cafe. The little guy behind you who was so worried about the state of your eyes is Griffin. The guy looking through his black bangs is Dannie Spain, king of the permanent wave. And Mam, my name is Tex. I come her every morning after cleaning offices. I'm sure glad to meet you. I'd feel mighty glad if you'd join us." Tex motioned to the chair between herself and Dannie Spain.

Mary gave Tex one quick look and followed the motion of the Tex's gallant hand. For one confused moment Mary realized that she wasn't sure if Tex was a cowgirl or cowboy. Then she decided not to think about that and just follow the friendly direction. Mary appreciated clear direction.

Shirley disappeared into a swirling huff, and the three companions followed Mary's suite and settled back into their chairs. Tex's few words were finished, and Mary felt high and dry. There she was surrounded by strangers, all looking at her as if she was supposed to say something. All she could do was wish she had never walked in the door. No matter how much she relaxed her hands and feet, no words came out. She couldn't even spread open the newspaper, because there were too many plates on the table. As her face prickled hot and the smell of bacon grease annihilated her senses, she heard a soothing, genteel voice next to her.

"Honey, so you're having one of those days too. Lordy, I swear if it gets any hotter, this wig of mine is going to shrink, and the whole world will see that I'm bald as the day I was born." He pointed up towards that furry contraption on his head and with a 32 carrot smile, winked.

Mary opened her eyes wide, sure enough there was

something odd about the way that hair perched on his head. Then she blushed because he caught her staring at his head.

"You go ahead and look honey. I'm a hair dresser. When I start on clients, they look like a mess, and I look pretty good. By the time I'm done, they look pretty good and I look like a mess. It makes them think they got a real good deal. But honey, this morning we both look like a mess."

Her three companions began laughing as if being a mess were a fairly delightful occupation. For the first time in months, maybe years, Mary found her face relaxing and something like a hiccup started coming out of her stomach; she actually began sneaking out a little laugh. She allowed her glance to settle on each of her new companions for a moment. Tex who had big breasts and a face like John Wayne mopped herself furiously while she laughed. Dannie's wig tilted genteelly but dangerously further toward his left ear. The third person, Griffin looked like some furry little animal that had just scrambled out of the gutter. He kept staring at her with glittering eyes.

Her mind stuffed with anxieties, choked off her laughter; she again found herself floundering like a beached whale. While everyone was crowding around looking at her, she somehow had to pour milk from her glass into her bowl. The muscles of her arms and shoulders locked as she froze in self consciousness paralysis. Finally she jerked into motion; it was now or never. She picked up the cool glass and with the precision of an engineer began very slowly pouring the contents of the glass into the bowl of corn flakes. Unfortunately she was pouring so slowly and carefully that some of the milk was detouring down the side of the glass. On the table was forming a white puddle that was just beginning to break its dam and trickle down into Mary's lap. She was being so intensely careful that she didn't notice a thing until she felt something cool dripping between her thighs. Her eyes opened wide in horror.

"That's a pretty nifty way of cooling off on a hot morning." Griffin who had been watching each of Mary's maneuvers, nodded genially in her direction.

For a second, placid Mary Blu wanted to explode into a frantic scream. That little man dragged her over to this table. Now he was making fun of her for spilling milk. Maybe it was the memory of Rita Reinke, she wondered why these little people are always getting her into trouble; how come? Like things aren't hard enough already without this pipsqueak forcing her to eat breakfast with a bunch of strangers. She glanced up at him; he was staring straight at her!

Tex very casually and quietly pushed the black metal napkin holder in Mary's direction. Mary plucked one, two, three, four napkins and followed the trail of the milk. She even gingerly placed a napkin over her crotch and shot a not overly friendly look at Griffin which she quickly covered up with an embarrassed smile.

He only caught the smile, and beamed with satisfaction. Griffin who hated familiar paths, had never seen someone approach breakfast with such originality. Why Mary Blu was wonderful. His toes were twirling, and he was just about to pour a little puddle of coffee onto the table, too.

Dannie's voice interrupted his delight. "Griffin Frank, you stop watching that lady right now! Can't you see that she's got enough to do without the likes of you watching her every move? Didn't your mamma tell you not to stare?"

Toes suddenly limp and smile collapsing, red started to seep into Griffin's face.

Mary looked at Dannie like she was a sheep found by a shepherd. He was dressed so wonderfully fancy too. The wings of her heart fluttered.

A bedraggle Griffin looked up at Mary. "I'm sorry if I embarrassed you Mary. I really WAS interested in what you were doing."

Mary took one look at the sodden napkins and the sodden look on Griffin's face, and wanted both messes to disappear. She mumbled something incoherently.

As if that were a signal of a happy ending, Dannie straightened his wig and said, "Honey, you just come by tomorrow morning, we'd love to see you again. You hear?"

Tex said, "Yup."

Mary smiled and successfully stuck a spoonful of cereal into her mouth.

Once again bustling with delight, Griffin popped up from the table as if he couldn't be restrained by breakfast any more. "I'd sure like to see you again too, Mary Blu. I like the way you eat."

At the sound of her name, Mary took an embarrassed gasp of air. Unfortunately she had just placed that spoonful of soggy cereal in her mouth. Her whole large form convulsed into waves of coughing until all the air around her was saturated with tiny droplets of milk and little globs of cereal.

The last thing Mary remembered was seeing one milky blob slowly begin crawling down the black napkin holder. She retreated to some private lair whose location even she didn't know.

Her solitude was interrupted by the sounds of chairs being pulled away from the table and footsteps disappearing. She was staring at her cereal from so close that she could actually see the corn flakes absorbing the milk. She hoped that if she watched closely and long enough, that slimy feeling between her thighs would dry out. She didn't even want to think about the little puddles of her breakfast that had settled on the table. That Griffin!

Without lifting her head, she slid the bowl of cereal out of her field of vision and slid the newspaper in to take its place. She crumbled and fluttered the pages open until she finally reached the employment section. Maybe it was her wet lap, but no matter how resolutely she stared at the print, she couldn't stop thinking about her latest fiasco. Even worse, tripping down a steep incline of memory, she fell down the pit of her accident prone past, leaving herself sprawling with all the painful reminders of her mishaps. She had no container in which to stuff all those memories. She no longer had the plodding regimen of her nursing career or the pressing need to take care of anyone.

Chapter 4

At twenty five years of age Mary had stumbled into a LPN nursing school. She had to do something; obviously she wasn't going to get married. Her hulking form roamed the hallways of that technical college for two years. All those other students, excited about the latest techniques for catheterizing patients' bladders, eventually became accustomed to her tiny little voice and larger, clumsy form. All her teachers whenever they discussed Mary would shake their heads and mutter how hard she tried. Her very last teacher, Ms. Tippy Rondheim spoke with Mary right before graduation. Tippy stared at her attempting to look past Mary's bumbling earnestness. Mary shivered and squirmed as she felt those eyes bore into her as if they were looking for something deep down. Was it resignation or mercy; Tippy finally smiled and suggested Mary look for low stress nursing positions.

And Mary did. Even emboldened by her white nurse's cap and the little gold pin with "LPN" printed on it, she was very cautious when she was let loose into the world of nursing. To her surprise, all she had to do to find a job was to page through the health care employment ads, carefully avoiding any ads that required technical skills or enthusiasm, and then circle insignificant, little ads. She figured the less elaborate the ad, the less elaborate the demands. Not that she didn't have a passion for taking care of people, but she didn't want to try to do something too complicated. That could lead to catastrophe; but no matter how hard Mary tried to follow Tippy's advice, catastrophe seemed to be the final destination of any job. The world of nursing clenched Mary into an embrace that first promised safety and then delivered disaster. In her last foray into nursing, she thought she had finally settled on an almost foolproof job at The Rainbow...

Mary's whole big body flushed all red and prickly at the table. She even forgot about the dampness between her thighs. She nodded her head until her nose was actually resting on the newspaper. Perhaps this time she'd better try a different profession. She lifted her face a little and forced her eyes to look back at the newspaper. Methodically she began at the very beginning of the employment section. Her eyes strained to study each mysterious employment category.

Advertising executives, attorneys, bass players... nothing seemed to fit. That's when Dannie Spain's face started to flicker in her imagination. That dark friendly face, the shiny turquoise shirt, those romantic black locks of his, tilting towards his ear; there was someone who needed the kind of reassurance that only she, Mary Blu, could give.

Maybe it was the unconscious but persistent dampness between her thighs, but for the briefest of moments she wondered what that long, slim, black body would look like without clothes on. Under the pressure of looking for a job, even more disturbing thoughts began popping up. She had actually never seen a younger man's privates. Sure, in the nursing home she had washed urine and feces off old men's bodies, but their genitals were retracted into mere nubbins. And even then she tried not to look. As for her father, she liked to think about that even less.

She could almost feel her father's underwear carefully folded at the bottom of that big box in her apartment. She knew they were probably there, because of that wadded up stained tee shirt that she had found newly erupted and huddled against the corner of the box this morning. Who knows what still lay lurking and unbidden there.

She stared blankly at the newspaper as she plunged into her past. When Mary was a child her father had worked at the stock yard splitting hogs. He would get up early in the morning while it was still dark. Mary would be awake listening. First she'd hear her mother creak out of bed and drag herself into the kitchen with a sigh as disappointed as cold oatmeal. Then her father would bound out of bed and into the bathroom, releasing a shattering stream of urine into the toilet. For some people the smell of coffee holds a promise, but not for the residents of the Blu household. By the time Mary got up both parents would be sitting opposite each other staring into coffee so cold and lonely that they didn't have to pour milk in to cool it down.

Her mother would tear her eyes from her cup and stare at Mary in bleak desperation, as if her mother were falling off a cliff and was looking to Mary for a last hand to save her. Her father simply stared straight ahead as if the worst had already happened. Then he would push his chair out, standing up not really straight, and walk out the door sentenced to some terrible fate. At night he came back, bent a little more and with bits of pig gore dried to his boots.

Mary hated Saturday afternoons the most. Her mother would roast beef or chicken, but never pork. She always over cooked that meat as if she were trying to delay the meal and what she knew would follow.

Mary and her sister, little Arlene, would finally be called to the table to chew the leathery meat. Their mother would serve everything in the slowest of motion, almost demanding that her daughters take seconds and thirds... anything to prolong the meal. Arlene never could eat much, but Mary would take seconds or thirds or even fourths, taking one more desperately offered serving.

Finally after that fourth helping, her father would shove his chair back, heading toward the bedroom with excited momentum. Her mother would start frantically cleaning up the table as if her frenzy could save her from what was about to happen next. The bedroom door would open. Her father would be in a sleeveless tee shirt with yellow stains down the sides. He wore gray boxer shorts shapeless over his hairy legs. He'd flop into the bathroom and pee so hard into the toilet that it sounded like thunderstorm. Then he'd usually fart and for the first time in the week heave a sigh of satisfaction. As her mother would clang louder and louder in the kitchen, he would step out of the bathroom and say, "Helen, you get in here right now!"

Her mother would freeze and immediately put down whatever she was holding. Tranced, she would walk toward that bedroom and without looking at her daughters would say, "Why don't you two girls go out and play now."

That's when Mary would take Arlene away, anywhere... under the cottonwood in back, or during winter into the coal shed, but most important she would take Arlene away somewhere in the stories of Mary's mind where people were hopeful and so gentle that they didn't even pick dandelions...

Mary now found herself in Surely's cafe clutching the newspaper with her large hands. She just knew Dannie wouldn't wear stained underwear and wouldn't do scary things with women. She erased any sense of Dannie's body and simply remembered how he had saved her from that Griffin today. Mary Blu felt something warm and soothing in her stomach; she wondered if this was what it was like to be in love.

She again spread out the newspaper and began examining the ads. The humid air of August, the sizzle of frying bacon, and yes, being in love...the morning looked back at her and smiled delicately.

"Hey doll, you done with that?" Shirley's hand was

already reaching toward the glass; she was never one to wait for long.

"Oh ya, I'm through Shirley. The cereal was real good."

Shirley's tightly wired form with mascaraed eyes bulging out as if something inside were trying to burst out, tightened to a standstill. "You gotta be kidding."

Mary who had never kidded anyone in her life blushed and swallowed air. Thank god it was air.

Shirley glanced down at the newspaper open to the employment ads. "Looking for a job, doll?"

Mary's whole body wilted banging her head into the newspaper on the table.

"Give me a look at those hands."

Head still pressed against the table, Mary stuck her hands out into space, turning her palms upward in sacrifice.

Shirley bent over the table and picked them up examining them in the light. "With mits like these you sure don't have to worry about Prince Charming coming around, but they'll do for dishes, doll." Then Shirley picked up the glass, bowl, silver, and that trail of wet napkins ending in Mary's lap with the rapid sweep of her more delicate hands. She spun around in a frantic pirouette and landed back behind the counter where bacon was beginning to smoke. "See you tomorrow at 8 a.m. You get free lunch, 10% of the tips, and all the second hand smoke you can stand."

Mary looked up resting her examined hands on her lap as she spread her large feet out under the table. "Ya, sure Shirley." Maybe Mary was in an altered state triggered by the surprise of good fortune; she looked up in Shirley's direction and smiled. "You've got a nice name Shirley. When I say 'Sure, Shirley,' it kind of rhymes. Did you ever notice that?"

By this time Shirley was whacking the burned bacon to the side of the grill with a huge metal spatula that rang against the griddle. With a casual sweep of her arm she pushed over a heap of sliced potatoes into the center of the grill. Without looking up, she wiped the sweat from her face and muttered, "You gotta be kidding!"

Mary forgot about the damp spot on her lap and simply sat there in front of the newspaper that now lay casually, unthreatening in front of her. What a morning! She'd get to see plenty of Dannie Spain, and that nice person Tex. Even Griffin didn't seem so bad. And she would be washing dishes, not just once and a while like at The Rainbow, but all the time now. She would be doing something, really doing something; not just trying to reassure people or pretend things weren't happening, but she would be doing a real skill, an art even. She Mary Blu would be doing dishes for a living.

She watched Shirley's body make precise, dramatic movements, like some beautiful dance, all angles and mysterious. Tomorrow, Mary would be part of that. She could go back to her apartment with a future. Maybe Roxanne would come over. Mary realized guiltily that she hadn't thought about Roxanne all morning.

Chapter 5

Griffin walked home that morning. Despite the lovely warmth and the freedom of a whole day before him, something under his skin was itching, and no matter where he scratched, whatever it was, kept itching. Walking up that sidewalk, past the shoe repair shop, this little man with wild coarse hair could be seen scratching his hands, arms, back, and legs. Mother's passing by with children shielded their faces as the little man even scratched between his legs.

When he got home as usual he tossed off his shoes, but instead of satisfaction, felt uneasiness. He threw off his clothes; his small hairy body fidgeted around the apartment. As a last resort, he scampered into the kitchen and poured some granola from a brown paper bag into an oversized bowl and sat nibbling at the window with a far away, blank look on his face, toes beating a frantic rhythm. Instead of looking at the wavy heat of the road, or hearing a small girl outside skipping rope and counting forlornly, he was in the grip of some problem that spun him around in dizzy circles.

That grip suddenly released and deposited him at the source of his dilemma. There across the street, sunlight hallowed in her frizzy grey blond hair, walked a large woman in absent minded grace. Not that everyone would immediately recognize it as grace, but Griffin did. He had an eye for things wild and ready to burst into life.

An undersized girl with oily hair held up with a pink barrette stopped her determined jump roping, and ran up to that woman and started talking non-stop. The large woman crunched down on her haunches and smiled back so warm and friendly that it could have turned a winter day into springtime. Griffin's heart broke then and there.

That's when he not only recognized that face, but what was itching under his skin...Mary Blu. He watched her and the little girl step into the house next door. He shook his head in disbelief; he and Mary Blu were neighbors.

Chapter 6

"I was trying to find you Mary. I yelled up a couple of times. I banged on the trash can too. Where were you Mary? Where were you?" Roxanne Crabtree's tight face squeezed out a whine. Mary looked down. When she recognized the familiar melody of fear, she crunched way down so she'd be at equal eye level. Roxanne's little face flickered, one minute cold and threatening, and the next all soft and hopeful...she was a child of many losses and few goodbyes.

Mary was careful not to look too long into Roxanne's face; there are things children don't want adults to see. Instead Mary touched a clump of Roxanne's hair that had escaped the dirty pink barrette that now was hanging in front of her face like a fish hook. Mary smoothed it out and placed it back behind Roxanne's ear where it wouldn't poke her eyes out or threaten anyone else. "Roxanne Crabtree, I'm planning to stay around here. It may not be forever, but I promise that I won't go away without saying goodbye."

Roxanne's whole little body began relaxing at the touch of Mary's hand, but as soon as Mary said something about not staying forever, Roxanne's eyes started to harden again into cold pebbles. "What can I do with a stupid old promise. You're gonna go away. Stupid Mary Blu!"

Mary settled onto her big haunches. "A promise is a funny thing. It's what you give to a person who you really care about, because you know sometimes things don't turn out the way you want. A promise is a way of telling a person you won't forget them no matter what. It doesn't mean I can make things turn out the way you want, Roxanne. It does mean that I'll always try to do good by you, as much as I can. And that's a promise." Mary's back end was slowly slipping closer to the sidewalk, but she so wanted to let her thoughts and words come together and ease out, that she didn't notice. Like a promise, she rested her eyes on Roxanne while Mary's whole big body was sliding downward in the slowest of motion.

Roxanne had an intent look on her face, like she was watching a television in a dark room. "When mommy wants me to do stuff, she promises me things. She usually forgets." Roxanne shook her head, and that hook of her hair jabbed back across her face.

"Those aren't necessarily my idea of promises, Roxanne. You can't make too may of them or make them too big, or else they don't mean anything. I know. I used to have two friends I worked with, and I kept promising to make everything all right for them. I guess I did that with everybody back then, but all sorts of horrible things happened, and I couldn't make it all right for anybody, even me. They got hurt bad, and I got hurt real bad. Now I try to keep the size of my promises down. I stand a better chance at keeping them." Mary smoothed out that hook of hair again and clipped it under the barrette.

Roxanne looked like she was listening real hard, so hard that she wouldn't switch the channel. She looked straight into Mary's eyes...a major accomplishment for Roxanne.

"Besides, Roxanne Crabtree, I have lots of reasons to stay around here. First, there's you, and then there's some other nice people I met today, and then there's this new job I'm starting on tomorrow, and then as if all that weren't enough, someone in the neighborhood plays the harmonica every night and lets me know it's all right being alone. I plan to be around for some time, and if I get ready to go, I'll let you know."

"So you won't go away without telling me, Mary. You'll always be here, unless you tell me? You promise Mary, you promise?"

"I promise Roxanne I'll let you know if I go away. I have some cherry cool aid upstairs in the refrigerator. Do you want a drink?"

"Wow, cherry cool aid just for me? Can I have some? Can I have a real big glass?"

"Sure Roxanne, but you'll have to give me a little hand." Her whole hunched body was wobbling precariously. Roxanne put out her hand. Mary reached for that little hand and delicately steadied herself. Then her two large legs caught their balance and pushed her up to her imposing height. "This job I got today is really wonderful.

I'm going to wash dishes at Surely's Cafe. I like washing dishes. I just do the same thing over and over again so I'll hardly make any mistakes."

Roxanne nodded solemnly. "When school starts maybe you'll help me with my multiplication tables."

While the two walked up the sidewalk to the big old house in which Mary lived, she scrambled in her purse for her keys...there she found them. The two walked up the sidewalk that someone had tried to patch with new cement. She paused in front of the gray metal door that had been patched into the entrance, fingering the keys for a few tense moments; she never knew which way to turn keys or even door knobs and usually had to try every combination of right and left before she ever reached anywhere...there, she had it. She pushed the door open and ushered Roxanne into the shadowy hallway. Roxanne touched Mary's blouse as the door clanged shut and closed out the day. This house was now cut up into little apartments for people like Mary who lived alone. The smells of cat litter and fried hamburger and much slept in sheets saturated the darkness. Not that Roxanne was afraid; she had learned long ago that being afraid was how the world seemed to work.

Mary turned to her right towards a whole shadowy row of waist high little metal doors. Each little door had a name taped under it. Mary took a tiny flat key and opened the box under which was written the name "Mary Blu." She stuck her hand into the little cavern and pulled out one lone letter. For a moment she forgot about Roxanne; even in the gloom the script on the letter was familiar.

Once again Mary Blu found herself slipping down the chute of her past. Those memories rushed in and filled her mind...sweet, sad, and even angry, those memories mixed together. She stood soaked in those memories: her dead parents, the old house, the garden, her nursing career, The Rainbow, Rita Reinke, Hernando, Ariane, but most important, Arlene Blu, her sister, her little sister. There on the left hand side of that envelope, clear even in the dimness was Arlene's name and address. The letter had been addressed to that dead end house of Mary's past; someone had kindly crossed it off and wrote her new address.

"Mary, it's spooky in here. Are you all right Mary? You look like you saw a ghost."

Mary looked at Roxanne from the distance of the past. Her voice took a moment to surface from those depths. "I'm okay Roxanne. This letter is from my sister Arlene. It reminded me of a bunch of people I used to know. She left for Alaska about the time things started to go real bad for me. Right before I ended out here."

Roxanne, at eleven was already an expert at being left behind. For a flash of a second she stopped worrying about loosing Mary and felt something new and softer from her insides. She touched Mary's hand and gave it a little pat.

"Let's go upstairs Roxanne; I'll pour you some cool aid, and we'll sit on the back stoop. While you drink I'll read this letter."

"You have a sister Mary? I wish I had a sister, then I'd always have somebody to play with."

Mary didn't hear, she was already pounding up the dusty wooden stairs.

After a few tense moments of key jangling and door knob twisting, the two stepped into the apartment; a surprise of sun was shining through the window into the living room. That room usually shadowed was soaked in the late morning light, floodlit like a stage.

Although Roxanne made a practice of not caring about anything, especially people, she was entranced by the big old bulging box in the center of the room. "What's this big old box, Mary? What's it for? What's it for, Mary?"

Mary looked over at it as if she had never really noticed it before. She was always too busy stuffing things back into it to take the whole thing of it into consideration. "It is a pretty big box, isn't it?" She scratched her head.

"But what's it for Mary. Why is it out here like this?"

For a while all Mary could do was keep scratching. If this had been anybody else but Roxanne, Mary's head would have started wobbling in confusion, but now Mary's big face began being animated with something like curiosity, and without even trying, words came out of her mouth. "You know Roxanne, I'm not completely sure what it's for. I found it in the attic of the house I used to live in, and that writing there on the side of the box is my mother's. I just brought it along. I've never even looked inside, but stuff has a way of kind of falling out when I least expect it. It's there in front of the window because at least I won't trip over it or spill any food on it."

While Mary spoke, Roxanne was edging her way closer to the box, and as if the suspense was suddenly too much she stepped right over to it and touched a little, old pink dress that looked like it had a red stain on it. "Whose dress is that Mary?" Roxanne held the dress up in the sunlight. She studied the dress. When she noticed that stain her face too reddened, but she kept staring at it like she was reading a book. "That used to be my dress Roxanne; I was even younger than you when I wore it. I was at a Sunday school picnic. We were having potato salad and coolaid and hot dogs. That's where that stain comes from. Some of the catsup from the hot dog slid down my chin and on my dress. The other girls laughed, and later no matter how many times my mother washed the dress, the stain wouldn't come out. I decided after that to never put catsup on my hot dogs or anything else, ever again." Mary's chest was moving up and down in little rapid-fire breaths.

Now Roxanne was staring straight at the dress and shaking her head. "That must be pretty hard to not have catsup. That's the only thing that makes food taste good. Sometimes for supper I make catsup sandwiches. My mommy doesn't care when I spill things."

Mary's face began melting into sadness. She wasn't looking inward or outward now, but in some middle space where she was no longer embarrassed. She stayed there for the longest time and then began making funny little snorting sounds that finally turned into a big relaxing sigh. She yawned.

"What are you going to do with all those clothes Mary? I bet you could do something with them."

And for the first time since that box had been dogging

her steps, Mary began wondering about what was inside. Just as she actually started considering what she would do with the contents of that box, a cautious look spread across her face and she decided she'd better get that coolaid for Roxanne. She fled to the kitchen.

Roxanne stared at that box for a minute, almost like it was some arithmetic problem. Then she peaked around the room of her new friend. She saw the sagging sofa with a yellow scarf draped over the corner of it. When she heard the refrigerator open she ran after Mary. "That yellow scarf is really pretty Mary. Where'd you get it from?"

Mary put the pitcher of coolaid down and stared out the window for a moment. "A friend gave it to me a few months ago; her name is Ariadne. It's a special scarf. When things get really bad, it's supposed to remind me that it's good to stop struggling sometimes."

By this time Roxanne's attention was captured by the big pitcher of bright red coolaid. Mary pulled out two glasses from the cupboard and poured them full.

They settled on the back stoop, all sheltered by the dusty August leaves and the drowsy sound of traffic; Roxanne with a big glass of coolaid, and Mary with her letter.

Dear Mary,

I'm sorry I took so long to write. I didn't want to bother you until I was a little more settled. I didn't want you to think you had to do anything to take care of me. Some nights I still wake up and think I'm in our old house at the end of the street, and in the morning I'll see you up already fixing breakfast. Then I realize that I'm in Alaska, and I miss you like crazy. But after I miss you like crazy for a while, I remember all the other things about living in that house on a dead end...the way I felt so trapped and how towards the end I blamed you for everything. I'm not proud of that Mary.

And just when I'm about to be overwhelmed by guilt and sadness, I hear Herman breathing next to me, and then I feel the warmth coming from his body, like a friendly hello that he doesn't even know he's saying. And then I'm back here in Juno, and mostly things are all right, or at least as all right as I've ever known.

Herman expects me to do things like cooking, taking care of the house, and tending the vegetable garden. I think he was surprised when he found out I didn't know how to do much. You always took care of things Mary. Sometimes he looks at me kind of confused, but not mean, like he doesn't know how a grown up woman has gotten through life without having learned to do so many things.

We drove in town to the library, I checked out all kinds of books on cooking and home economics. You know how much I like to read. I wanted to buy subscriptions to cooking magazines, but Herman said that he doesn't have enough money. And he really doesn't. He has this farm, except it's way out in the woods. He also traps a lot of things and sells the furs for money. He shoots deer and moose and animals I had only seen in National Geographic specials. Then, with a few things we buy at the store, vegetables from the garden, and those strange dead animals; I'm supposed to make a meal.

Believe it or not, I'm doing all right with that.

Fortunately Herman appreciates how hard I try, not just how things taste.

I am a little worried about you, Mary, being all alone. I wish there was something I could do for you, but my hands are pretty full and I need to be away from you for a while.

I did press some flowers for you, and I hope by this time you have already noticed them in the envelope. Even with all the vegetables, I still grow flowers. I also wrote a little poem to send to you. I don't have nearly as much time to write, but I hope you'll like it anyway. I remember how much you like movies.

> Might as well
> Step inside the movie.
> The story
> Is the pulse
> Of my own blood.

Still Your Sister,
Arlene

P.S.

I'm sorry I didn't have time to make it rhyme, but maybe that's not as important as it used to be."

And Mary could feel her own blood boil, a throbbing, except it didn't hurt. She noticed the pink dried flowers in the fold of the letter spill out fluttering to the ground. Then she looked at a patch of green poking out of the tarred ally below. A small white butterfly, the kind you see in cities, quietly flickered through the summer air and settle onto a solitary dandelion. Then its wings stilled. When Mary squinted her eyes, she saw it sticking its long delicate nose into the heart of a dandelion on that summer day. She looked and paused so long that it seemed like forever. The butterfly finished and flicked away.

"So, Roxanne, you're learning multiplication tables. I had a hard time with those but I finally learned them. When school starts, I'll give you a hand."

Chapter 7

Mary got up while the morning was only a faint glow in the east. The leaves on the cotton wood stirred fitfully, and one lone car drove up Franklin Avenue with its lights on. Today was the beginning of her new career at Surely's. Mary wasn't exactly sure how dishwashers are supposed to dress, since it was a behind the scenes role. Maybe they wore uniforms. She thought about wearing her nursing uniform, minus that little white hat; but decided that those tight whites would be too restrictive if she had to do a lot of turning and lifting. She had always bought uniforms that were a little tight; she thought they'd make her look smaller. Now that she hadn't worn any of those uniforms for some weeks...

Just as she was becoming frozen in anxiety, she noticed a pair of her fathers overalls hanging over one end of that troublesome box. Instead of jumping up and stuffing that intruder back in the box, her face softened into bewilderment and then curiosity. She started making tiny little slow steps toward the box as if her feet had lives of there own. Her eyes kept getting bigger and bigger not in terror but in wonder. Now her hand was easing its way to the box. Wonder of wonders she touched the overalls and wasn't struck by lightening. Then she picked them up and backed toward the sofa. She lowered herself into the arms of the sofa and spread her father's overalls across her knees. She sat there in her own personal dawn.

Finally she looked straight at the overalls as her fingers began feeling the denim. The blue material was still soft and worn with a kind of friendly give, so unlike her memory of her father. Best of all, they didn't smell of pig gore, but of some pine smelling detergent. Before she even thought about it, she kicked off her slippers and inserted her large feet and legs into commodious space of those denims. Her whole body spread out in ease. She felt like those broad legs of hers had finally found a place that matched their size.

Barefoot she sauntered around the living room in her new getup; she did refuse to look into the mirror though. Finally she settled on a pale pink, ladylike blouse that buttoned high up on her neck; and of course her sensible white nursing shoes. She liked the spongy soles even though they added another inch to her already towering height. When she stepped out of her apartment that morning she turned around anxiously for only a moment wondering if thgis is what people called an adventure.

The morning had cooled down some, in fact if you gave yourself time, you could feel just a hint of cold, but

Mary wasn't concerned about the end of summer when so many things were starting new in her life.

She joined the crowds of quiet people rushing to work, feeling part of something, not just of the crowd of people, but part of the whole morning. Even a block away from Surely's, the smell of bacon and syrup tickled her nose. For a moment, her stomach flip flopped and she faltered, as if she didn't deserve to be a part of this wonderful happening. Then she looked up and saw Dannie Spain in the cafe window straightening his wig in a hazy mirror above the counter, and suddenly the day seemed worth the risk...she smiled.

Even though Dannie was pretty involved with trying to look his best, he caught her delicate smile as she walked in. "Hey Girl, you look cool as a cucumber, but you have to do something about that hair of yours. You have a big face, honey, and you need to soften it."

Mary stood next to him, taking all those words in. No one had ever talked about the way she looked, at least not in front of her. She was a person for whom people had more practical uses. She blushed as she realized that he was actually looking at the details of her face. She hardly ever looked in the mirror and when she did, she blurred her eyes so that she could just get a general sense if she was presentable. She felt that if people looked too closely they were sure to spot something disturbingly out of place, maybe even grotesque. Quickly she hung her head down to blur Dannie's view.

"Honey I can do miracles. You need curls. Here's my card. Call me and I'll set up an appointment."

Mary tilted her head up slightly and said in a tiny voice, "Sure Dannie." She clutched at the card and almost touched his hand. His finger nails were all shiny and long. For a moment she wondered if all black people's nails were like that, then she became so overwhelmed that somebody liked her, even if she had to make some changes.

Just at the edge of her vision, she noticed another pair of eyes looking at her with a frightening glitter. Griffin was looking straight at her as if he wanted to say something or even worse, do something. He cornered her eyes; that big head of hers that was beginning to tilt downward, drooped towards the floor. She mumbled, "I better go see what Shirley wants me to do."

She noticed Tex out of the corner of her eye. She looked up long enough to glance in Tex's direction and then returned to more pressing concerns. Tex minded her own business. After spending most nights cleaning people's offices, she preferred during the day to let people clean up their own messes.

Someone else was watching with more than casual interest. Though Shirley continued slapping down plates, pouring coffee, and exhaling smoke; her eyes never left Griffin's face. She saw it flush and dazzle at Mary.

Now most people said that Shirley wasn't a bad sort. She had been one of those little girls who desperately tried to be smart, popular, and pretty; but rarely succeeded, although that never prevented her from trying even harder. Not a bad sort, especially if you didn't interfere with one of her plans.

Shirley Wiggles had been born in Minneapolis and

by the age twelve, had already become the star little dancer of Miss Francine's School of Dance and Feminine Comportment at the intersection of Franklin and Park. Shirley had found an arena where she could pit her not always graceful determination against more lack luster classmates. Her brown ponytail could be seen frantically bobbing up and down across Francine's dance floor every afternoon after school. Her wiry body strained to kick and spin, challenging the lone image of herself in the wavy wall length mirror.

One afternoon a week, Miss Francine joined Shirley, playing the piano and shouting orders. "Higher, Shirley, Higher! No, not that way Shirley Wiggles, you look like a frog…with charm, more lady like. I'll show you doll." Then Francine would interrupt her pounding version of the Dream Of Love and stand up with the self conscious grace of a queen. Urgently she'd spring into motion, waving her long thin arms and kicking her legs high; so high that her voluminous red velveteen skirt would open like some huge red flower.

Shirley's adoring eyes would grow big as the sky as she watched the gypsy queen swirl red with bracelets jangling.

Francine would have her glittering eyes fixed on the mirror. "Now that's how it should be done, lady like, charming. That's the way we do it in New York!"

Shirley would shiver in excitement, and imagine herself spinning, maybe, someday maybe, even more beautifully than the gypsy queen. For the next week Shirley would spend even longer hours at the dance studio, comparing the frog like vision of her self with that ladylike image of her teacher. One day Shirley started wearing bracelets.

Perhaps in payment for that adoration Miss Francine bestowed on Shirley a very special privilege. Shirley had a co-staring role in The Miss Francine's School of Dance and Feminine Comportment's Yearly Recital. All the more lack luster little girls would dance in a sequinned unruly mob to The Nut Cracker Suite. But the best part was saved until last. Miss Francine would perform her own choreography based on the story of St. George and the dragon set to her old standby The Dream Of Love. She danced the role of the beautiful maiden threatened by the dragon, and that's where Shirley came in.

All dressed up in purple tights, with a long black tail, and a frightening Frankenstein mask; Shirley would charge around the stage, while Francine would swirl and smile at the audience. St. George had been cut out from the dance all together. Finally the dragon and the audience would be totally disarmed by the maiden's glamour. Shirley got hot and sweaty under all that costume though. When she did actually get a chance to take the mask off and bow, well, she didn't look very ladylike.

By the time Shirley was eighteen, she too wore long dresses and learned how to bang her bracelets loud enough to get most people's attention...for a while. Though her strained face never relaxed enough to be pretty, she compensated with generous amounts of make up. Blood red lipstick formed an illusion of luscious lips. Her eyes already popping out with effort were outlined in bold strokes of black. She plucked out her eye brows and penciled in two little dark fish that seemed to be always swimming towards each other only to be stopped by a deep vertical crease above the bridge of her nose.

With the wistful blessing of Francine, Shirley set out for that city that doesn't sleep, New York; unlike sleepier Minneapolis it matched Shirley's frenzy. She moved into a tiny one bedroom flat with three other girls as determined as she to hold center stage. She auditioned for dancing roles on Broadway, Off Broadway, Off Off Broadway, and finally settled for road shows of HAIR and OH CALCUTTA! where she had chorus roles in which she took her clothes off and writhed with as much lady like charm as she could muster. And then she couldn't even get those roles. More and more of her time was spent as a waitress in a small Polish restaurant on the Lower East Side. There, finally, with swirls and bangles she held center stage, surrounded by hungry patrons impatiently waiting to be served their meals.

During this period she had various boyfriends: punk rock musician wannabes, actor's who spent more time studying themselves in the mirror than she did, and out of town business men who paid periodic visits to New York and put up with Shirley's charms for the price of a cheap place to stay.

One morning when she woke to find her current boyfriend and all her electrical appliances had vanished, she decided that it was time to share her glamorous talents with people who would appreciate them; she moved back to Minneapolis.

There she started working at the Sleepy Eye Cafe

and eventually took it over as her own domain, calling it Surely's. There she met Tex, Dannie Spain, and Griffin. She showered her charm on all of them. In fact she had a brief affair with Tex, after all Shirley was very sophisticated. The affair continued until she discovered that Tex really didn't like to clean up other people's messes, no matter how glamorous.

Next she cast her net on Dannie, but was disappointed to find that they were rivals in the quest for men's attention. Finally she settled on the least promising of the trio, Griffin. Despite the effort she took to dress him up in designer jeans, over priced running shoes, and Italian shirts; he never was able to live up to her standards. She discarded him with a certain wounded longing.

Betrayed by Griffin's indolence, at forty she began saving her charms for her customers and perhaps for some impressionable, fortunate neophyte who needed molding. She, Shirley Wiggles would be a lone valiant beacon of true glamour.

That very day, Juan, her dish washer, got his green card and deserted her to work at an expensive Japanese restaurant downtown, that great unfinished lump of a woman, Mary Blu, stumbled into Surely's. Now there was a woman who really tried. And so Mary Blu became part of Shirley's plans. Besides Griffin needed to be taught a lesson: if he was going to be gallant to anyone in this restaurant, it better be her. That night she ordered a subscription of THE GENTLEMAN'S QUARTERLY and had it anonymously sent to Griffin's address. Shirley indeed was not a bad sort.

"Hey doll get over here. There's work to do. This isn't one of those health spas!"

Mary scrambled behind the counter and into the kitchen.

Shirley made her more glamorous entrance through the swinging door and into the kitchen, giving Mary a once over. "You gotta be kidding with that outfit! You look like a lumber jack in drag! You may not have much in the looks department, but if you hang around here long enough, you'll see how a real lady dresses."

Mary wasn't sure what drag was, but it did sound like Shirley wanted her to stay around, and Mary liked to be needed. She nodded her head.

"Gotta hair net?"

Mary's head drooped, as she realized that she had already made a big mistake.

Shirley was in a forgiving mood. "Never mind doll." She reached toward a stringy, black mess draped over a nail pounded into the wall. "Here take this; it was Juan's, it'll suite you. Your no beauty queen."

Feebly Mary reached over to take that mysterious wad of black thread out of Shirley's hand.

"Come on doll, stick it over your head."

Mary fumbled with the black mesh, and finally opened it pulling it over her frizzy hair and halfway down her forehead. A big black knot perched right above her nose.

Shirley appraised her charge and nodded with satisfaction. "That's better doll."

Mary was relieved.

"Now doll your job is to do these dishes. When you

get done with these, you go out without making too much of a scene, and grab the dishes I leave on a cart by the counter. Now let me introduce you to your new boy friend." Shirley walked over to a waist high, metal box that was huffing steaming. It sat next to a counter and two deep sinks all piled with dishes. "Here's how to use it doll." Without actually touching the dish washer, Shirley began a dramatic pantomime, as if she were actually using the huffing machine. Her flowing skirt swirling as she pointed and prodded and danced the instructions for her amazed pupil.

Mesmerized Mary watched Shirley's grace and wondered if her own towering and not so graceful form could carry and crunch and swoop and lift with such mysterious style. She could almost feel the buttons of her tight blouse popping. Well, she'd just have to do it.

Giving Mary one last dubious look, Shirley swirled out of the steaming kitchen and returned to her more glamorous side of the swinging door.

Mary was left to the towers of dirty dishes and the enigmatic dish washing machine. At first she tried to remember all those fantastic, beautiful movements of Shirley's, but that didn't help. Memories of disasters from her life filled with disasters, began rumbling through her body. The past with all its crushed opportunities began avalanching down, overwhelming her with icy terror. Her whole body was being frozen and crushed. She was suffocating; only her eyes could move, staring out in panic under the hairnet. Maybe it was all that steam huffing into the room or the memory of what her friend,

Ariadne, had taught her about letting go when things seem impossible; Mary's whole form began softening and finally loosening. She started defrosting, and finally her knees began reluctantly creaking as she walked over and actually touched her mechanical companion. He blew steam out reassuringly.

In the thaw, she began mixing her memories of dish washing at The Rainbow with some of those mysterious movements of Shirley, and some sort of inner animation began moving through her, maybe even intelligence. She set out to explore. Before she knew it, she had soap and a tray full of dishes in the machine. She pressed a button; for a half a second nothing happened, and then miracle of miracles the machine shuddered and she could hear a rotary arm start to spin and hot water spraying over dirty dishes. She gave her friend a tiny pat, and moved over to the counter to examine another tray of dirty dishes.

By the end of the day those dungarees were soaked with sweat, and they definitely didn't smell like laundry detergent anymore. Her sodden pink blouse was opened a third of the way down her chest. A tiny bit of bra strap peeked out. Her body was tired but it hummed with all that lifting and swooping and crunching and reaching; she forgot how she looked.

There...she slid out the last load of dishes. She, Mary Blu, had completed her first day of work without a major mishap, at least none that she knew about. She was so tired that she didn't even care. She pulled the wet hair net off, hung it on a nail to dry, and pushed through the swinging door.

The restaurant was empty except for Shirley. She was counting dollar bills while a cigarette drooped out of the left corner of her mouth. Occasionally she'd interrupt her concentration by clenching the left side of her face and taking a deep drag. "Get over here doll and get your tips."

Mary stepped over obediently.

Shirley blew out smoke from a kind of funnel she made on the right side of her mouth, Mary was in its path.

Enveloped in smoke, Mary was so excited about the money that she swallowed smoke and all. Her whole body exploded in coughing. She couldn't even squeak out thank you.

Shirley took another drag from the cigarette hanging from the left side of her mouth. "Hey doll, you got TB or something? If you're gonna cough, cough on the patrons. I don't want anybody else's diseases."

Without thinking Mary stepped out of Shirley's line of fire, grabbed the money and fled before she could contaminate her boss again. The last thing that Mary heard as she walked out of Surely's was, "I keep my word doll, just ask anybody. See you Monday, same time, same place."

Surely's was closed on Sundays. She wasn't interested in those stuckup people who stroll around pretending that they are people of leisure. This wasn't a Sunday sort of place; besides she needed her beauty rest.

Chapter 8

It wasn't just triumph that Mary carried with her as she headed home with long, excited steps. First she was going to call Dannie and see if he could see her tomorrow. She fingered the damp paper card that held Dannie's magic phone number. She also carried a more vague intent with her. What was it now...oh yes; she'd look through that box to see if there was anything else she could use in her new life.

Roxanne was already positioned on the steps to Mary's house. While waiting for her friend she had taken a thick piece of blue chalk that she stole from school and had written "MARY BLU, MARY BLU, MARY BLU" on the sidewalk leading from the stairs all the way down to the boulevard. Roxanne was now sitting on the edge of one of the steps to see if her little bit of conjuring would work. And who should come walking down the block but Mary Blu.

"I made you come Mary. I kept writing out your name over and over again. I knew you'd come."

Mary was feeling pretty pleased with herself anyway, but to be welcomed by a smile, well that was happiness beyond Mary's imagination. She stopped and stared at the sidewalk with her name printed again and again, as if she couldn't quite understand the connection between those carefully printed "MARY BLU's" and Roxanne making her come.

Roxanne was so excited that she stood up with her fists clenched. "Don't you understand Mary? Don't you understand? It's like when my teacher makes me write a hundred times "I WILL NOT SQUIRM," and then she knows I'll try to be real still unless the boy behind me starts poking me. I thought if I write your name a bunch of times and wait a little, it'll happen too and you'll come. Especially if I actually use blue, just like your name. It worked Mary, it worked!"

Mary scratched her head trying to make a connection to magic, but then she noticed how carefully her name had been printed out in big, beautiful, blue letters. She decided that it was one of the nicest gifts that anyone had ever given her. She walked over to Roxanne, careful not to step on and smudge any of the blue. She touched one of Roxanne's hands and it uncurled all soft. "It's beautiful Roxanne, you're real artistic maybe even magical."

For a moment Roxanne squinted her eyes in suspicion. She had learned to guard herself from what people said about her, all the names she had been called.

Mary's body crunched down again to be on Roxanne's level. "My sister Arlene is artistic and maybe even magical. That means you can look at something that other people think is ordinary and see all kinds of new and beautiful things you can do with it. Who would ever think that a sidewalk could be so wonderful!"

At the word "wonderful" a smile snuck across Roxanne's face. "I'm just like your sister...Mary?"

"You sure are. But I've got a surprise for you. You know that big box upstairs with all that stuff in it, well I'm going to look through it this afternoon. Do you want to help me? There might be all kind of surprises in it. Maybe we could use some of that stuff."

"Maybe it's like a treasure, Mary. There might be diamonds inside and lots of gold. Lets go Mary, hurry, c'mon."

They both raced to the door and for once Mary was too excited about getting somewhere to try to remember which way she should turn the key. Like magic, the door opened. They ran up the stairs so fast and loud that doors all along the hallway opened a few inches and frightened eyes peered out. The two friends hardly noticed.

Roxanne didn't even ask for coolaid; she just ran right up to the box and stared at it. Mary was right behind her, breathless. They studied the big box, eyes opened wide, as if they could hardly believe that they were finally going to get to see what was inside. They stood motionless for a few moments, then Roxanne began squirming. Mary closed her eyes and slowly lowered her hand into the box. She left it there for a moment. By this time Roxanne was jumping up and down. Finally Mary grasped a hold of something and pulled it out of the box. She opened her eyes. It was another pair of dungarees. She stared at it for a minute, blinking her eyes. There had been so many new things that day; she seemed to be getting into the swing of surprises. She looked over at her fellow explorer and nodded her head. "I can use these for work next week. It's your turn now Roxanne."

Roxanne's hand was already perched above the box. Her body stopped bouncing; she closed her eyes and stuck her hand in too. She pulled out a purse all shiny and green, with a little pearl clasp on it. When she opened her eyes she could hardly believe the wonder that she held. "Can I have it Mary, can I have it?" She burst out with excoitement, "It's so beautiful!"

Mary's big face opened into an easy smile, as if finding treasures was the least they could hope for this afternoon. "My mother gave that to Arlene when she was going to go to the prom. She never went because she got sick. Arlene had a way of getting sick before she was supposed to go out. But you should have that because Arlene was artistic too. I bet you could put your chalk in there."

Then both of them began grabbing things out of the box. There were some poems on scraps of paper, some old photographs, a little wooden box full of threads and needles and a pin cushion in the shape of a turtle; but mostly there was just raggedy clothes, Clothes that nobody would ever really want to use. There was even a pair of blood stained underwear that Mary hid after she had her first period. Of course she didn't know that it was a period back then; she thought she was bleeding to death, maybe because she touched herself down there too much. One day while Mary was hiding down in the coal shed waiting to die, her mother found the underwear under Mary's mattress. A little bit of rust red cotton had been peaking out from under the mattress. Objects had a way of tripping Mary up.

That's when Mary's mother told her about the curse. Mary was relieved to know that she wasn't bleeding because of some particular thing that she did wrong. Her mother solemnly told her that the curse was the punishment for all women for tempting men. Her mother wasn't real clear about what the temptation was all about, but was real clear that Mary should cover herself at all times, and keep away from men. She could only be with a man if he were her husband and she his wife, and being a wife meant that she had to do whatever her husband said…no matter what.

Roxanne caught Mary staring at those panties. Very matter of factly Roxanne said, "My teacher at school said girls bleed into their panties when they grow up. It has something to do with making babies. Since I don't want babies, I've decide not to do it, I mean bleeding."

Mary dropped the panties in the pile for raggedy things that no one in their right mind would want. In fact when the box was completely empty there were two piles. One very little pile consisted of the purse, the dungarees, the wooden box of sewing supplies, a bag of feathers, a communion veil, her nirsing cap and a few of Arlene's old poems. There was also a very big pile of raggedy clothes.

"What are you going to do with all that stuff Mary?"

"I don't know, I suppose I'll put it back in the box. It seems funny my mother wanted all that stuff saved." Mary shook her head at that pile of rags. "Well, why don't I get us some coolaid. We deserve it."

Mary and Roxanne sat on the sofa drinking coolaid staring at the pile of their dashed hopes. Finally Roxanne said, "The purse is really beautiful, I'll use it for all my artistic things."

Mary kept shaking her head. "It still seems to me that all that stuff must be for something." She put the sewing box on the kitchen table; she carefully folded the poems in the communion veil; but never did get around to putting the raggedy stuff back in the big box. That unruly pile of clothes took up what seemed like a permanent residence in the center of the room.

Chapter 9

For Mary, this was a weekend of necessities. True, she had discovered another pair of dungarees to wear, but all those shiny, high buttoned blouses of hers clearly wouldn't do for dish washing. Not that she had any notion of style, but the blouse she had worn Friday had popped three buttons and at least two seams. After a day of work, Mary Blu had stuck out all over the place.

Saturday was the day for necessary enterprises. Most of the stores on Franklin Avenue had been turned into coffee shops or used record stores, but Lake Street, ten blocks away had never bowed to the tattered chic of Franklin Avenue. There were still grocery markets, a big KMart, and several stores where you could cash checks. The street had once been the beating heart of a Scandinavian neighborhood, but after the Second World War those blond descendants of northern Europe began fleeing to the suburbs. At least those descendants young enough to flee.

Wave upon wave of new people began settling on the Street. Black people from the South began migrating up to taste northern freedoms and prosperity. Hmong people all the way from South East Asia began fleeing to Minneapolis; this street was a haven from slaughter. Mysteriously Indian peoples from Southern Mexico began appearing. Somalian women swathed in gorgeous colored clothes roamed the grimy street like exiled butterflies. Clean, orderly, busy, blond Lake Street now was multi-hued, chaotic, and sometimes dangerous, but it pulsed with extraordinary life. There were children from all over the world who had there first taste of the American dream in the McDonalds and Burger Kings and Arby's that popped up all along the strip, or at least the sections of it that were safe enough.

Mary felt at home in that area where people played music loudly and looked as lost as she. With small, timid but determined steps she walked from Franklin to Nicollet and headed straight down to The Street. The world became stranger and more interesting the further she went. There were so many oriental grocery stores that she lost count. She passed Vietnamese restaurants, taquerias, and even a Mexican bakery. She stared in the window at all the brightly colored cookies. Scandinavian bakeries had been more somber. The streets were full of people walking in an out of stores with bags; most of the busy people were shorter than she. Right before Lake Street, Nicollet dead ended at the KMart Store. It was like a dam that she had to walk around to get to the KMart entrance on Lake Street.

And there it was, Kmart standing like some shabby

cathedral. It swarmed with mothers and squalling children. Young swarthy men clustered in groups around the front entrance waiting for the girls in tight shorts pulled high on their hips to promenade by in giggling two's and threes.

The girls usually only bought cokes or trays of tortilla chips swimming in gooey cheese. The mothers walked out of the store pushing grocery carts filled with formula and disposable diapers and cheap children's clothes stacked high.

Those young men hardly noticed Mary's big shapeless form, besides Mary's mind was focused on serious things especially those fried chips with yellow goo. She could almost taste the crunching salty taste in her mouth. Saturday morning at KMart; it was like paradise.

She walked into that busy cool cathedral, awestruck, and found a grocery cart to push around. She wondered through the aisles looking at the toys, children's clothes, radio's, and even at the shiny golden chains behind glass. This was what Saturday morning was meant to be. That's when she noticed the Star Trek tee shirts all tossed together in one big pile on a counter marked "SALE." Not that she watched Star Trek, but she loved the way the Star Ship Enterprise stood out all bright against the black preshrunk outer space of the tee shirts. Most important though, the tee shirts came in extra large sizes.

She picked out five of them and urgently headed straight to the cashier; she had something even more exciting waiting for her. She even forgot about the chips.

Yesterday as soon as Roxanne left, Mary called Mr.

Dannie Spain. As a special favor to her, he said he would squeeze her in on Saturday. The very mention of the word squeeze made Mary flush with excitement on the other end of the line. She imagined Dannie's glossy finger nails caressing her hair. Her mother had always cut her hair with a matter of fact abruptness.

Mary marched out with all those other pleased customers carrying precious bags. She headed down noisy Lake Street, past the last remaining Scandinavian bakery that now advertised fresh tortillas, past the store with the big sign "All Checks Cashed," past the bus stop where a child was screaming, and finally there it was... MR. DANNIE SPAIN'S HOUSE OF BEAUTY. Without hesitation she pushed open the glass door and walked in. One woman was sitting in a chair with a strange buzzing helmet over her head, and there was a funny smell like the time her mother cracked an egg open that was too old. Most important, there stood glistening, satiny, and slightly disheveled Mr. Dannie Spain who was bending over a woman looking at her head as if it were a work of art, and he, Dannie Spain, was responsible for it.

Mary Blu took one deep breath of that rotten air and squeaked out, "Hi Dannie" over the buzz of the helmeted woman.

Dannie glanced up reluctant to be disturbed as he placed his last finishing touches on his triumph. Then he recognized Mary's head bobbling form and said, "Honey you got in here just in the nick of time, hair like yours can cause accidents on the street! Sit yourself down, and I'll be right with you." He motioned toward an empty chair.

Mary released a sigh of relief; she had enough accidents in her lifetime, and if some new one could be avoided, she'd be grateful. She stood there patiently aware that for once she had avoided an accident.

Manwhile Dannie swiveled his female masterpiece around on the chair, grabbed the cloth lying so smoothly on her shoulders and swirled it off. She stood up looking all fresh and complacent. She handed him some crumbled dollar bills. Then he banished her.

He walked over to the woman in the buzzing helmet, lifted that contraption off her head and motioned her over to the chair of honor. There he pulled out plastic sponges from her hair, his face taut with suspense. Then he began combing her hair out all the while gasping in wonder at the miracle before him. Dannie spun the chair around and that woman with ravishing hair gave him money too before she was banished into the world.

Then Dannie bowed towards Mary and gallantly waved her into the empty chair.

He looked at her with sympathetic disapproval. Like some daring toreador, he spun a red plastic cloak over her body, but Mary was already conquered. She docily followed his lead to a sink over which she hung her head. There he ran warm water through her hair and poured on a little shampoo. Just when Mary thought that things couldn't get more wonderful, Mr. Dannie began working his fingers through her hair with a sensuous circular motion; occasionally the tips of his shiny finger nails would nip little kisses into her scalp. She fell into Dannie's artful embrace.

Finally Dannie stopped and motioned her back to the other chair saying, "Honey you have to stop using bathroom cleaner on your hair." Her whole lower body was now Jello with little waves quivering through it. She knew she'd follow him anywhere. There...she made it into the chair and back into his hands.

Without further ado he took his comb and scissors and began his new masterpiece. While the scissors nipped around Mary's head, Dannie's voice lullabied her. Although occasionally he paused to casually watch one of those swarthy young men saunter by. "So you're new to the neighborhood honey? I sure hope everybody is treating you fine. All of us get down on our luck sometimes. Why I remember times I was so far down I hardly knew which way was up. Then before I knew it, I was back on the top of the world again. Like my mamma says, 'Get, while the getting's good. You never know how long it's going to last.' So honey, I hope you're going to get some good and enjoy it for a while. Why after this haircut you're going to look so fine, people are going to stop you on the street and ask you for your autograph. And you just tell them that Mr. Dannie Spain had a hand in it."

He paused to watch a young man walk by with a plaid shirt hanging wide open. While the plaid waved in the summer air, sweat was rolling down the young stranger's heavy chest, past his belly button, and into a furrow of hair that stretched mysteriously and compelling down into his pants.

"How you doing today honey?

Mary pulled herself up from a pool delight to answer.

"Well, ah, things are going pretty well. I got that job at Surely's, and I met you, and there's this girl named Roxanne who lives next door..." The sound of the chattering scissors in her ear encouraged her on. "I do have one little problem. I brought this big box of stuff with me from where I used to live. I brought it along because my mother wrote 'SAVE' on it. My mother's dead now; so I saved it."

Dannie stopped looking at a little bull of a man charging by the window. "Honey, I'm sorry your mamma's past." He looked straight at her shaking his head and making a kind of sound with his tongue against his teeth like locust make at the end of the summer.

For some reason Mary almost started crying, but she snorted the tears back. "You know Dannie, I looked in that box and there was mostly raggedy stuff that nobody would want to use again. Stuff that me and my family wore a long time ago. I don't want to throw it away, but I don't know what to do with it."

Now, Dannie not only saw himself as a hair stylist extraordinaire, but also as a cross between a councilor and an plumber. His job was to listen, all the while clipping away, and then give advice that would free up anything that was stopping up his clients' lives.

For a moment he forgot about the parade of male beauty at the front window. Even that snipping sound paused for just a few moments. The beauty parlor was fraught with suspense. "Why honey it's important to do what your mamma says..." There was another pause. The scissors started snipping with frantic rapidity as if some pressure had just broken loose. "Why, Mary Blu there's no need to get your panties bunched up by a box of rags. Do like my momma did. Why, she used to save old rags, and in winter when we couldn't do much in the fields, she'd cut those rags into long strips an inch or so wide and make braids. You know how to make braids, honey?"

Mary nodded. She remembered how she used to braid Arlene's hair that summer when Arlene wanted to be an Indian princess.

"When my momma would get all those strips of rags in a pile at the center of the room. Then she'd take three strips and make it into a braid and shape it into a tight flat circle so it would lie flat on the floor. Then she would sew it tight. Then she make another braid and ring it around that circle. She'd sew that tight onto the center. Then she'd ring another braid around that making sure it was sewn and tight, and still flat on the floor...and then another braid and another braid spiralling like a wheel on the floor. Like magic it would start becoming a technicolor rug. The spiral would get bigger and bigger until the braids were all used up. Presto! One minute she'd have a pile of sorry old rags and the next thing I knew, it would turn into a beautiful rug."

Maybe it was Dannie's humid breath on her neck, but somehow she thought that she, Mary Blu, could make something that would be beautiful. After all she had plenty of rags, and she could braid, and how many mistakes could she actually make if she just kept placing that braid round in a circle and sewing it? Seems like she had a whole lot of practice going around in circles.

Mary felt herself being spun in the chair. There to

the music of Dannie's oohs and ahs she saw herself in the mirror. By some sort of magic her hair had turned from wiry grey blond mass to shiny curls all over her head, like a halo. Her mouth dropped open big enough to contain a flock of geese getting ready for their flight north.

"Honey, with hair like that you can really strut your stuff!" Mr. Dannie whipped the red plastic off Mary Blu and said," You go girl!" He winked. "This ones on me."

Monday she reported to work as prepared as she had ever been in her life, the Star Ship Enterprise heaving on her amply bosom, prepared for take off. Maybe it was all that swooping and lifting, but over the next few weeks, she developed a certain economy of motion while she did dishes. No longer just an anxious imitation; something from inside of her own body seemed to be warming up. Extremities and organs once perched haphazardly on that jumbled form of hers to be jarred loose in any confrontation, began finding some inner principle of unity. Her self coalesced around her idiosyncratic Dance of the Dishes. There was one casualty though. The constant puffing of steam in the kitchen soon transformed her artful coiffure into a wild mass of gray blond hair even frizzier than its previous state. After first apologizing to Dannie, she collected her bouncing mass of hair with a rubber binder and created a spongy ponytail. Despite the grid lock of her fears, something unbidden but welcome was springing up in her body that started at the tip of her toes and pushed all the up to her braided ponytail...at least when she was in the kitchen.

Besides, she had an important enterprise during those

evenings that kept shortening. While the harmonica music played she'd grab another piece of clothing from the pile in her living room and carefully cut it into strips. Roxanne had wanted to help with this, but for this task, Mary wanted to be alone. One day she'd pick up an old yellowing white shirt of her father's; the shirt he wore to go to church on Christmas Eve. Normally he wasn't much for church but the family had to leave the house long enough for Santa Claus to come. Her father usually left church for a smoke right before the very long sermon. He'd get back right before the priest blessed the congregation and shooed them out of the church. Another day she'd pick out an old dress of her mother's that had faded flowers on it. Mary could hardly remember a time her mother wore any thing but brown.

Each evening she'd pick up memories from the past. She'd look at them, feeling them with her fingers, and sometimes even smelling them. Then while the harmonica music played she'd sit alone in that room in the evening. Finally something would seem to spark her from the inside, and she would begin cutting. She thought the sound of scissors slicing through the material sounded like the last of the crickets outside.

That fall, she would bound out of her house, banded bushel of hair bouncing, dungaree clad, and The Star Ship Enterprise in motion. That big face of hers looked straight out from a body that some people could even describe as handsome. Mary was happy.

With new purpose, she walked out into the world on that Monday morning in late September. Frost coated the sidewalks and each individual blade of grass, but even at 7:30 a.m. the sun was turning the frost to dew. She loved the way the smell of rotting leaves mixed with the car fumes of Franklin Ave. Her feet grasped the round ball of earth below her and she spun it round. Occasionally people noticed and even turned around to look at that big striding woman.

Mary Blu walked through the door of Surely's, familiar with the smells of greasy food and the clatter of silverware. Familiar, that's what she felt. She even pulled up a vacant chair and sat next to her...friends? She had never actually known anyone before who she didn't have to take care of.

She tilted her face up and looked straight at all three of them, even Griffin, and finally let that smile rest on Dannie.

Tex who appreciated a handsome woman was the first to speak. "You look mighty fine this morning Mary."

Mary's head maintained its straight forward look, even under the barrage of appreciation. "Why this morning is so beautiful, Tex. I just could have kept walking for hours, like I didn't need anybody, just me and the morning."

Tex blew out a breath that ended in a chuckle. "I love to see a woman who takes care of herself. It tickles me."

Mary's head began bobbling a little. She glanced at Dannie to see if he liked the way she looked.

Dannie cleared his throat. Lately he had noticed that no matter where Mary Blu was in a room, her attention was usually on him. He wondered if just maybe there was a little misunderstanding. He smiled back at Mary apologetically like his wig might be slipping again.

Mary, well she only saw a tender irony, a romantic detachment, like here was somebody who would love her but never need her.

In the midst of that delightful misunderstanding, a voice rose unbidden. "How are you this morning NEIGHBOR?"

Mary dragged herself away from Dannie and turned toward eyes that always seemed to poke at her as if they wanted something...Griffin. She knew she needed to be nice. "Ah... neighbors?"

"I live next door, Mary, in that brick building right next to yours. Sometimes I see you with a little girl. I've thought about hollering hello to you, but you both seem so happy together, I didn't want to spoil it. How about stopping by some afternoon, when you get out of work; I'm usually getting up from a nap at about that time. I'll put on some tea and we can get to know each other a little?" His stubby, hairy fingers were drumming on the table.

She glanced at Dannie so he'd know that she wasn't being unfaithful to him.

Dannie cleared his throat again and nodded a little frantically trying to redirect her attention back to Griffin.

With resignation Mary followed that direction. "Well I suppose so, sometime. I better get back to the kitchen." As she stood up she knocked the table, cups and saucers jangling; coffee lapped over brims. "My fault, oh my fault. I'm sorry, sorry my fault." Her whole body separated into confused parts. Worst of all she was afraid Dannie would be disappointed in her...that Griffin!

As she was ignominiously retreating an insistent voice tried to pull her back. "How about this afternoon Mary?"

The room was spinning around her. Her head began bobbing up and down frantically.

"That's great Mary. You'll see my name down by the door. Just press the buzzer. I'll be there." He slid a little piece of paper across to her. She picked it up automatically.

Mary made good her flight.

While pouring coffee and collecting tips, Shirley was spying on the whole conversation behind the camouflage of cigarette smoke. For the briefest of moments her bravado and even her charisma wilted. That taut face sagged, and even her swirling purple skirt drooped and deflated. Her eyes settled on Griffin and hardened. She'd have to do something about this, for Mary's sake. Yanking away someone's half unfinished plate, she followed Mary into the kitchen.

Mary was already springing into motion by the dish washer.

"Hey doll, how about staying after work today. When it quiets down here, you and I can talk."

"Ah, Shirley, I'd sure like to. You've been so good to me, but there's this thing I have to do. I don't really want to, but you know I promised, and a promise is a promise I suppose. But thanks a lot.

That funny drooping came over Shirley again. Then she tightened. "How bout tomorrow doll?"

"Sure Shirley."

Chapter 10

One load of dishes after another, Mary forgot about Shirley and even Griffin. It was just her and her steaming friend. The first few days of work, she had felt like she was placating a fiery dragon, her body scrunching and straining in capitulation. Sometimes she did the same load of dishes once, twice, even three times; afraid that she had forgotten the soap.

One day while stretching and pulling and bending, she forgot to be afraid. In fact she discovered a rhythm. She wasn't watching herself anymore, watching for missteps that would prove some final unworthiness. Mary Blu found herself dancing, not mysteriously, but practically; no need to be saved from that fire breathing machine or even to seduce it. Hair dampened across her forehead like seaweed, a steam of enchantment in her eyes, she moved with idiosyncratic grace. She liked her companion, its rotary arm spinning inside, steam seeping from the door, the smells...soap, bleach, the traces of breakfast food, and even the aroma that clung to her body in the slick coating of sweat.

4 p.m., she squatted down and opened the dish washer door. A contented huff of steam poured out. She lifted the last load of clean dishes onto the counter. With the resolve of a tender goodbye she poured a little vinegar into the bottom of the machine, closed it gently, and pressed a button. Those faithful arms spun one last time for the day, rinsing themselves. She wiped off the counter and sprayed down the tubs. The dish washing machine clicked off. The steam cleared to reveal her engagement with Griffin. She was too contented with herself to be irritated with her neighbor, besides no one had ever invited her to their home for a tea before.

She pushed through the swinging door and picked up her tips from the lunch counter. Something about the way Shirley was whacking potatoes with a huge knife, Mary decided not to interrupt her. Shirley's face squeezed into a squinty eyed grimace as she heard Mary saunter through the door. She heard a voice of warning following her out the door, "Watch out babe, he'll disappoint you. You'll see; he'll just use you."

A cool autumn wind patted Mary's face; she sprung down the sidewalk walking straight into the setting sun. While other people were fleeing from work to home, Mary stopped and closed her eyes; for a moment she wanted to be nowhere and everywhere: in the sound of a school bus whining to a halt, in the smell of a fall afternoon with a chill coming on, like Arlene used to smell all sweaty and sweet when she walked through the cool to get home after school; but mostly the way the sun burned through Mary's closed eyelids and doused herself and the whole world in orange. Only a few people stopped to stare at the big woman standing motionless in the sidewalk with her eyes closed and a smile on her face.

She opened her eyes to a blue beginning to turn cold. She moved on ahead towards her rendezvous, finally stepping into the chilly shadow in front of Griffin's building, her stomach started to flip flop, and her feet faltered for a moment. She stopped, took a deep breath of the cool air, and told herself that this visit wasn't very important. It's not like she was visiting Dannic. She stepped into the dark building and pressed the button marked "Griffin McGee."

Mysteriously the metal door buzzed, and she grabbed the handle for dear life and pushed it open. Smells of pot roast and old carpet reassured her. Her eyes opened wide and looked out like full moons for the stairs leading upward. The blood was simmering in her head. She was visiting somebody, a man, no errand of mercy to guide her.

The stairs climbed to her right. The worn carpet snaked up those stairs to a landing with a large dusty palm tree and a window looking out toward her home next door. On tip toes she ascended to the landing and touched the palm tree leaving a smeared finger print in the dust. Her blood was boiling now. She took another deep breath and began the final ascent. There, she reached the summit.

She timidly peered down the hallway; another smaller, nervous face stuck out of a beacon bright doorway. In an instant both pairs of eyes seemed to catch each other in an ambush.

Griffin let out a little squeak and then managed to collect himself enough to say, "Come in Mary." He made a gallant motion toward his open door.

Mary's left toe managed to get caught in the carpet and she stumbled into the apartment. Her considerable forward momentum was finally stopped at a big overstuffed chair. She toppled down surrendering to it, looking up hopelessly at her host.

He was dressed in a shirt so white that even in the hallway it shone. He had blue jeans on so clean that she could smell the detergent. His thick gray brown hair was slicked back like he had just taken a shower. Mary liked things clean, especially on men. She tried not to notice that his shoes weren't on.

He stood next to the chair and put his hand out to hers, a brown, hairy hand, stubby fingers writhing with excitement. She lifted up her larger more tentative hand and laid it in his. She felt his hand tighten around hers and release. A little sigh somehow seeped out of her, and she offered him an embarrassed smile. He caught that secret sigh and his bare feet began prancing on their own.

From his standing position, he looked down on that large form jumbled into the chair, and he bent down to catch her eyes and his nervous smiling face tilted downward. "What a pleasure to have you here, Mary!" And he let out a sigh so deep and full that both of them began laughing. On Mary's part the laughter was strained, but still it tittered out.

"Why don't you come in the kitchen and keep me company. I'm almost done fixing supper. Nice chair isn't it?"

She collected all the parts of herself splayed out on that chair and followed him in the kitchen. Somewhere in the hallway, she noticed almost reluctantly that even though his legs were short, they looked very strong. In fact now that his feet had stopped digging into the floor, his furry body seemed animated with a ferocious liveliness, like a cat. She decided not to think about that. What was it that Shirley had said?

But the kitchen was bright and filled with wonderful things that she had never seen before. There were shiny pans hanging from hooks on the ceiling. Bowls of all different sizes and colors looked out from shelves that lined one whole wall. On a small wooden cupboard sat a dark brown irregular pot, all knobby; and in it stood flowers and grasses. For a moment she thought of Arlene. Near a large window with smoky looking woodwork all around it, stood a small red and white table on which lay a real table cloth. It shone white as Griffin's shirt. Two plates rested on that pristine cloth, and they weren't just any plates. Tiny fish leapt all around the borders of these dishes. Mary knew the fish weren't real, but when she blurred her eyes, they seemed to swim. Pieces of matching lustrous silverware sat on both sides of the plates. Mary had only known dull forlorn pieces of silverware for which she could never find matches. On one side of the plates stood tall, clear sparkly glasses. On the other side were cups on saucers. One cup and saucer had blue and yellow flowers weaving in design over them. The other had a little cottage painted on it with a garden all around.

In the middle of the kitchen, illuminating these marvels, hung a light with a silky, yellow cloth shade with red fringes hanging on the edges. Inside, the light bulb made the whole yellow cloth shape glow like a rising sun. Mary had never seen such wonder in a house before.

Maybe it was all that beauty, she realized that she was very hungry. The apartment was filled with smells, subtle mixings; no packaged macaroni and cheese here. The fragrance steaming up from a pot on the stove filled her nose and drew her straight forward. Her face, her whole body moved wafting on that current. She was a welcome guest in someone else's house. For a moment she didn't even notice that she and Griffin were looking at each other straight on.

Then he began stirring the pot. "Well, I thought you might be hungry after a day of hard work. I made some chicken soup and dumplings. I have some peppermint tea here too. Do you like tea?" He looked doubtful for a moment.

"Oh, I like almost anything. I don't think I've ever had peppermint tea before; I thought it was just candy... but it smells real good." She caught his doubtful eyes and poured another smile into them.

"And for desert, if you want, I have oranges." He pointed proudly to a bowl on the table. In it were two of the biggest orangiest oranges she had ever seen. The setting sun was hitting those two lustrous balls resting in the bowl. Maybe it was the heady smell of chicken broth or peppermint tea, but Mary had a flash of intuition. "Griffin, I think I understand...that's why they call oranges 'oranges,' because they're so orange. Or maybe even better, they call 'orange' orange because of oranges."

Griffin was looking at those oranges with a born again intensity as if he were understanding some new revelation. He looked up at the prophetess. Then precisely at the same moment, they both remembered to be embarrassed. Falling from grace, Mary's head bobbled as if the pleasure of this afternoon were too much for her meager senses.

Griffin was in a different sort of quandary. As he was looking at her shining in the afternoon sun, he caught the aroma of her large body perfuming the air, a certain smell that reminded him of aching happiness; the way he felt in the evening, but he could play the harmonica then. Now he could only feel the impossibility of finding words to describe that tenderness.

"I guess I better check the soup. Do you want to sit down, Mary? Do you want tea now? Maybe you want to read the paper? Are you tired?"

So many questions were being fired at Mary that all she could do was stand there and hope somebody would tell her what to do.

Griffin wondered what he had done wrong and silently returned to stirring the soup.

Finally she sat next to the bowl of oranges for comfort; they seemed so simple. She stared out the window, emptying herself out of the line of fire and away from that person who seemed to want something from her that she didn't understand. She knew Dannie wouldn't be like that. He would smile in that mysterious way of his and begin talking to someone else.

A very composed Griffin began putting things on the table. While he was moving back and forth he quietly muttered reassurances to himself.

First came the tea pot, white with blue markings; Mary thought it looked mysterious like some ship captain might have brought it from some place far away like China. When she was a child her mother would boil water in a pan and drop in a tea bag and bunch of sugar. Even without the tea pot it was pretty exciting, because tea was something she didn't have to drink, like milk. She drank it for the sheer pleasure of tasting tea, even in the somber Blu household.

Then Griffin placed a basket on the table. Mary Blu had seen Easter baskets before, but this wasn't Easter. This basket was filled with thick slices of dark bread. The crust looked all hard, but inside was a surprise of dense, moist softness. Mary knew, because when Griffin's back was turned, she touched it.

Finally he brought out the biggest bowl that Mary had ever seen, at least she thought it was a bowl. It was shaped like a big fish whose belly was filled with fragrant soup. On one end was a tail flipping up, and on the other end was a fish face with two bubble like eyes. The fish looked like it was about to smile. In this strange land of new sights and smells, she took reassurance from that hint of a smile. Besides her stomach was churning, and saliva was rushing into her mouth. She wanted to eat; how simple things were.

Griffin sat down. His tight uncertainty was melting in the steam from the soup. He loved soup. Mary watched his nostrils flare, sucking in the aromas as if nothing mattered except this moment of pleasure that he had created. It scared her a little, and then she too was overwhelmed by the steamy smells filling the room.

"That soup tureen is from my great, grandmother McGee. She gave it to me before she died. She always put it out when I came to see her. Sometimes she put jelly beans or potato chips or even soup in it. She knew I loved to stare at it." He laughed at first a little apologetically, but then that laughter caught a hold of him, and his whole small body began shaking.

Mary, who at that very moment had been staring at the fish, felt something shivery ripple through her. She could picture little boy Griffin staring at that big fish waiting for it to wink back. Without even lifting her head, she knew Griffin was watching her stare at that fish too. Just then some tide rolled in and carried the body of Mary Blu out into laughter, rolling tears of laughter that kept carrying her farther and farther out into an ocean that she had never visited.

Griffin watched her while his laughter bubbled up easily.

Mary's laughter was another story. It began engulfing her. The more she tried to stop laughing; the more she seemed to sink into swelling laughter. The more she sank; the more she struggled. The more she struggled; the more she laughed. Laughter kept crushing in on her, heavier and heavier until she couldn't breathe. Her stomach twisted and ached as she struggled to pull in air. Tears squeezed out of her eyes, and she couldn't stop. She kept being pushed further out as each successive wave of laughter pounded against her and spun her deeper. She was tumbling down strangled by laughter. As her chest began caving in, a choppy wail of a voice came out of her mouth. She was so afraid that she put her hands over her face to prevent anyone from seeing her.

Griffin was watching her closely, laughing with steadier eyes. Finally he got up out of his chair and while tears and choppy moans were squeezing out of Mary, he stood up and stepped behind her chair, reaching around her middle in a firm grasp and said, "Now Mary you go ahead and laugh; I'm right behind you so you won't burst into pieces.

Mary felt those arms encircling her and let out a huge yowl of a laugh that set dogs barking for miles away. At first she thought she had died, but then she noticed that some strangling pressure had released in her. She could breathe again. The wild tide of laughter was moving out leaving little giggles behind. Her whole body began making little soft, sobbing sounds, snorting up air. She noticed that her face was wet. She felt one final cool tear meander down her right cheek and plop down onto the snowy napkin on her lap. She watched that tear soak in and form a darker spot on the whiteness...she made another mistake.

Griffin quietly walked back to his seat.

Even when she tried so hard, something always seemed to sneak up on her and make a sorry mess of whatever she was doing. "Oh Griffin, I'm so sorry. I didn't mean to laugh like that. I never cry. I'm so stupid to do that!" She took her hand and wiped her cheek, examining the moisture with throbbing embarrassment.

Griffin's face turned soft as the evening. "Well it looks to me like you haven't laughed for while, like it was all saved up, ready to burst out. You looked so beautiful Mary, all that coming from your insides."

Mary had never heard the word beautiful used to describe anything about her. She put both her large hands over her face and allowed her eyes to peak out of the lattice of her fingers.

"Why don't you try this soup before it gets cold. Here let me laddle you some. It's good for what ails you."

Mary began focusing herself around the simple task of handing her bowl to Griffin.

"Here let me pour tea for you too."

She held up her cup and saucer covered in blue and yellow flowers. Unfortunately this procedure wasn't so simple; for Mary at least, it was a feat of balancing. She had to hold on to that flat saucer and keep the cup quiet on top. The more she tightened her hand on the saucer, the more the cup rattled. She was so afraid of dropping and breaking her precious load. She imagined a look of horror on Great, Grandmother McGee's face."

Griffin watched the painful procedure. "My Grandmother McGee used to say that everyone gets at least seven mistakes a day. Doesn't matter if they're big or little. By the end of the day if you haven't made your share of mistakes, why, you haven't lived."

While Mary was distracted trying to figure out how anyone could say that she was supposed to make mistakes, Griffin poured the tea in her upraised cup. Before Mary knew it she had safely landed that cup and saucer back on the table.

"Please have some bread, Mary."

At least this time she didn't have to worry about breaking something. She grabbed at a large piece of bread and pulled it to her plate. That's when she noticed that she had taken the biggest piece of bread. What if Griffin had wanted that piece? Just as she began pushing that generous slice of bread under the rim of the bowl to hide her greed, the accumulated smells began overwhelming her: the chicken soup that smelled like Thanksgiving and Christmas combined, the peppermint tea that tickled her nose like a flower, and the yeasty bread as moist as a summer night, all seeped through her customary caution and sabotaged her with delight. For a few moments food was all that mattered.

She watched Griffin take a piece of bread and then dip an end into his soup; he tore off that chunk with his teeth and smiled. Mary did it too, even with the smile. "Do you like to cook much Griffin?"

"I get by pretty well. I like food, almost any kind as long as somebody has put a little care into it. I like to make food for people, especially for you Mary." The way he said Mary, it sounded like a breeze rushing through a cotten wood tree on a warm summer night, the sound of green whispering in the night. She picked up her spoon and dipped out a dumpling, like a tiny heavy cloud, except it had little bits of green in it. She dropped it in her mouth, and her teeth bit down into that soft spongy dough that tasted like chicken and perfume and heaven. Finally she took a sip of her tea, just because…the taste of peppermint seemed like it would be fun. Now she was too busy tasting and swallowing to have time for thinking, let alone talking.

Then Griffin patted his stomach and tilted himself back in his chair like he wasn't even afraid of falling. He nodded at Mary. "Where I come from, people like food," as if that explained the delights of the meal. "Mary, come on in the living room. Make yourself at home." He stood up and stretched as if he were rising out of a pool of delight.

Perhaps it was the heady influence of the peppermint tea, but Mary liked the way he stretched out, all easy with himself, even that little bit of hairy stomach that peeked out at her. His hands which she barely remembered had held her around her waist, now grabbed the bowl of oranges and a teaspoon. Somewhere during the meal, he had rolled up his sleeves.

Queasy and excited Mary noticed how hair curled around his strong arms and down his wrists, even reaching his fingers which were always too busy playing with whatever they touched to poke at her in punishment, even when she made a mess. As she wobbled to a standing position and almost tripped on the chair, she remembered with a little lapping giggle that she had a few more mistakes to make to fill her minimum quota of seven. She shouldn't have a problem with that.

She steadied herself and for a moment felt not only big

but grand. "Griffin that was the most wonderful meal that I ever had in my whole life." She began wobbling a little again. "I ah, really didn't expect you to make a meal for me or anything like that, you know it's so much trouble." And now she was having some trouble negotiating around a small round table with a very fragile lamp on it. She made a big loop around it and then lumbered into the living room after him. He sprawled out on one end of a large green sofa, and she slowly lowered her bulk onto the other end. There, she made it. She could manage to remain sitting here without too much danger of mishap.

Little did Mary know that the excitement of the evening had just begun. As soon as they settled in, Griffin's bare feet began making beating sounds on the floor. His nostrils began flaring as if he were on the verge of another delight. He edged towards the center of the sofa, creeping closer to Mary.

Mary's stomach tightened as she edged away slightly.

His arm sprang out toward the table in front of the sofa, and he grabbed an orange from the bowl. While his feet were now making a wild thumping rhythm, he rolled that ball of an orange between both his palms, squeezing it just tightly enough to release a hint of orange fragrance into the room. He looked at Mary with the same sort of look her father would have on his face when the family returned from Christmas Eve services...Griffin picked out a teaspoon.

He had her father's arms. She edge away more decidedly.

Whistling a little tune, he delicately poked at the

orange with the teaspoon and slipped the bowl end under the skin. The air exploded with the smell of orange. He pushed. The curve of the teaspoon matched the curve of the orange, and as if by magic the skin began sliding off in wide strips. Mary could hear a soft pulpy, tearing sound. That smell of orange sweet and spicy brought her back to the room. Her body relaxed.

Well, she couldn't believe her eyes. She generally avoided any food that took much coordination and effort to eat, and here Griffin was pealing that difficult looking orange like it was fun. Her mouth hung open in amazement.

Griffin noticed that large yawning cavern. "Haven't you ever seen anyone peal an orange like this before?"

Mary blushed and closed her mouth. "Ah, it looks so easy like it's not even a lot of work. Mostly I drink that orange juice that comes in a carton; all I have to do is shake it a little."

"Do you want to try your hand at it?" He pointed to the other daunting looking orange.

"Oh, I don't know. It looks pretty hard...I'll just make a mess."

"Well, Mary Blu, have you made your quota of mistakes today?"

Mary shook her head and began laughing almost easily.

"Why, this may even be a chance for bonus points. Here let me show you." He slid over to her end of the couch with the spoon and the orange.

In all the excitement she didn't notice his close proximity.

"Now this won't be bad. Are you right handed Mary?"

Mary's face froze and her head began bobbling. For her whole life she had been plagued by right and left. Anyone who knew her for long soon gave up the frustrating effort of directing her in either direction. Geographic movement was almost impossible for Mary since direction was a cruel joke, and she was its butt. Griffin watched wobbling Mary sinking into confusion. Just as she was about to drown, Griffin searched out her wavering eyes and in a flash tossed the orange to her. She was so startled that she simply caught the orange with her right hand.

"Good catch Mary; I think you're probably right handed. That whole right and left thing can be pretty confusing. It's not like north and south; some place that stays put. Right and left moves around so much that sometimes I don't know where to find it. Like now, my left is over by the arm of the sofa and my right is by you, but if I stand up and turn around, the sofa would be by my right and you would be on my left. It's a lot more confusing than people give it credit for. I think of right and left like too personal pets. The one named right is always by my hand that scratches my head. The one named left is by my hand with the little mole on it. Do see the mole? Now, if someone starts talking about right and left and I'm not sure if they mean my pets or theirs, I ask them to point."

Since Griffin scratched his head at every opportunity he could find, Mary saw where his right was; and the mole even though it looked like something on her father's arm, sure made the location of his left pretty clear. She understood him; she actually understood him. She was so excited that she couldn't speak; her face opened to some new kind of curious intelligence, a hesitant renaissance. "I understand where your right and left are Griffin, I really do." Then doubt began tightening her face. "But I don't have a mole and I don't scratch my head. My mother said scratching isn't very ladylike." As Mary spoke her voice gradually shrank into a doubtful, wavering whine.

As Mary became more daunted by the dilemma, Griffin's feet began pounding again, not in frustration but excitement; there was nothing he loved more than a good dilemma, except maybe for oranges, or summer mornings, or Dannie and Tex, or fat snow flakes falling, or Mary Blu...

Even Mary began to be infected with the momentum of his pounding excitement. She ventured out into the unknown. "I've been cutting all these clothes up for the last couple of weeks. I do it every night after supper while I listen to someone playing the harmonica somewhere in the neighborhood. I always hold the scissors in this hand. She pointed to the hand holding the orange. So my pet, Right, is always my scissor hand. I always hold the cloth I'm cutting up in my other hand." Her face was becoming more radiant with each word. "So my pet, Left, is in this hand." She patted an invisible pet with her empty hand. Her whole face was opening up like a sky after a dark storm, light bursting everywhere. "And all I have to do to know where my right and left are is to pretend I'm cutting cloth. And if anybody wants me to go to the right or left and I'm not sure if it's my two pets they're talking about, I'll ask them to point." She smiled as big as the blue sky.

Griffin was overwhelmed, all he could do was thump his feet and laugh. Finally he gathered himself together enough to continue with his lesson of pealing.

He spoke very slowly but with complete confidence. "Now Mary Blu, put the orange in your left hand."

And she did.

"Now pick up the spoon handle with your right hand. Turn the spoon over and rest that empty curved part on the curve of the orange...That's it." He slipped his arm across her back to reassure her.

She looked startled.

"You don't have to hold the orange and the spoon quite so tightly...that's it Mary. You don't have to think about it."

She nodded hesitantly to him. Her body shuddered ever so slightly and relaxed enough to follow directions.

"Now, follow the outside curve of the orange with the bowl part of the spoon. There that's it; just follow it around a little while like the spoon is going for a nice little ride, and remember, this is a chance for bonus points. There you go. Now without thinking about it, dip the end of the spoon through the skin; keep pushing it in until you hear a funny puncturing sound and then follow the inside curve of the orange."

Mary was really doing pretty well riding that spoon around the orange. It was as easy as washing dishes. But now she actually had to stop going in those reassuring circles and push the spoon through the rubbery surface of the orange. The more she thought about this radical endeavor the more impossible it seemed. To make the situation even worse she was supposed to stop thinking. The orbit of the spoon became more and more unsteady until it screeched to a frantic, rigid halt. Her whole life flashed before her eyes.

Griffin's hand gave Mary's shoulders a delicate touch.

The flashing story of her life began slowing down, her pulse settling…she plunged the spoon into the orange. She heard a puncturing sound followed by a more ominous squishing sound. Suddenly the closely peering faces of Mary and Griffin were showered with a fountain of orange juice.

While Mary's whole body crumbled in embarrassment, Griffin began bouncing up and down in absolute delight. "Congratulations, that's wonderful. You did it Mary, you did it, and besides you get bonus points!"

Mary's head which had been hanging down like a sheep going to the slaughter, peaked up at the sound of Griffin's delight. The force pushing her head down began releasing. She licked some sweet orange juice off her lower lip and a smile of delight stole across her face. She had done that, yes, she had done that, and she got bonus points too.

"Now this time, I'll have you go easy. Follow the outside curve with the spoon, and very gently sneak the spoon through the skin softly as if you are slipping under the sheet as you go to bed."

Mary pretended she had a big orange bubble in her hand. With each orbit the bubble became more real. She closed her eyes and without even thinking, her hand, with a delicate flip of the wrist, slipped the spoon under the skin. The little puncturing sound followed by silence was her signal to begin making a smooth curve around the orange. She opened her eyes. Like magic a wide peal was falling away. She was doing it. Once and a while after that her face would get all squished with anxiety, and she would get carried away and push too deeply, squirting juice, but Griffin would only grin at her...bonus points. Somewhere before that long, wide peal at last plopped from the orange onto her lap, she knew in her big boned body that she, Mary Blu had accomplished something.

Griffin removed his hand from around her shoulder.

While the peelings rested spent on the their laps, Griffin and Mary stuck there thumbs into the centers of their oranges and opened them up like fleshy flowers. Griffin didn't even have to tell Mary how to do it. Soon they were both chewing orange slices contently, orange juice exploding in their mouths.

The last slice of orange exploded in her mouth and trickled down her throat; she looked out the window and noticed it was dark. Night tugged at her, that shadowy place filled with frightening surprises. She noticed the messy peel on her lap and that her body sat big and lumpy in the sofa. She was sure that she didn't smell good, and why did Griffin have to sit there smiling as if he were waiting for her to do something? Didn't he know that doing anything usually meant disaster? "Well, ah, Griffin, I suppose I should go now. Things tasted real good, and I really liked being here and all, but I think I better go home now. I have to work tomorrow, and I better go home."

Griffin's smiled flickered for a moment, but not with

the kind of sadness that hardens into disappointment. He looked at her with soft, steady eyes like he did when she couldn't stop laughing. "I'm glad you came Mary Blu. I think you're fine just the way you are."

Now there was another word she had never heard to describe herself..."fine." People had said that she was nice, but that usually meant people wanted her to do something. Fine was different; it confused her. She yanked herself out of the sofa; funny how she seemed stuck in the sofa, like part of her wanted to stay put. Finally that dark uneasiness inside of her succeeded in pulling her up. Her whole body was at cross purposes and she was barely able to glance an apologetic smile at Griffin. He placed a hairy hand on her knee to steady her. Her whole body tensed up as hard as a stone, then fled his apartment leaving a little trail of fineness behind her that only Griffin could see.

That night while she cut rags, whoever played the harmonica on Franklin Avenue, played it especially soft and sad, like it was a melody wooing the night.

Chapter 11

At 7 a.m. when Mary left her apartment, cars on Franklin Ave. still had their lights on. The air was so gray that it turned people on the sidewalk into scurrying shadows; she could hardly imagine that last night all those wonderful, brightly lit things happened. She blew out that memory into the bone chilling air, and it became a cloud disappearing into the gray. She walked towards Surely's with funny, disjointed steps. One second she'd stroll ahead thinking about chicken soup and oranges and the next second she'd pause thinking about hairy arms and her father's stained tee shirts…so many jangling things that didn't fit together.

She opened the door and saw three familiar faces looking up at her, glad to see her.

"Howdy mam." Tex winked.

"At first I wasn't sure about your au naturelle look, honey, but it suites you." Dannie straightened his own not so "naturelle" wig.

Normally Mary would have tried to wring every bit of attention out of Dannie, but today she was in too much a of quandary about herself, to dream about someone else. Mary did peek down at Griffin, and his eyes were staring at her as brightly as those head lights outside. The smoky yellow lit restaurant started spinning around, facing swirling, geography and time mixing up. Her stomach flip flopped like when she tried to read in the car when she was a child, her father's hairy arms clutching the steering wheel. She learned to put the book down and not try that again.

Griffin's face turned the color of a strawberry and he started scratching his head with his right hand. He lifted his left hand, the one with the mole on it, from under the table and pulled out a single red rose all encased in shiny stiff plastic. "I stopped by the SuperAmerica on the way here. I thought you might like this."

Queasily she turned away from those staring eyes and that hand, and even that rose. No one had ever given her a flower before. The room spun faster until it was just a blur and she was alone. She closed her eyes.

Dannie's voice brought her back to some semblance of geographic steadiness. "Hey honey, this weather's getting me down too. Back home it would still be summer."

It took her a moment to figure out what exactly he was talking about, creating time for her stomach to settle. She knew she needed to do something, after last evening and all. Her stomach did a little flip again. She focused her attention on trying to help Griffin. After all that's what she did best.

She steadied herself, yes, helping Griffin. There he stood looking confused and forlorn clutching that rose that was meant for her. The least she could do was be gracious, like her mother used to say, "When you feel cornered, be gracious and do what you have to do."

With her long practiced nursing condescension she picked the rose out of his hand, glancing a disjointed smile at her suitor. Of course she wouldn't smell the rose, that could set off the room spinning again. She would do her head bobbling best for Griffin, yes, for Griffin.

Griffin's face was now as read as the rose. He looked away. The whole restaurant seemed to quiet with suspense. What would happen next?

From the direction of the grill, a loud "whack" woke up the room. Shirley shot a hostle glance at Griffin and smiled with cold satisfaction. They locked eyes for a moment. And life started clanking forward again: someone ordered bacon and eggs, a man got up to bring his bill to the cash register, and Mary fled towards the kitchen.

Right before she disappeared through the swinging doors, something in her body stopped her, her feet wouldn't let her disappear. She turned around and glancing at Griffin said, "Thank you Griffin. No one ever gave me flowers before. I've seen girls get flowers, but I thought I was one of those people who just wasn't supposed to get them. Um, not that I needed them or anything."

Griffin, huddled in his chair looked up and caught her gaze for a single instance, long enough for him to say. "That's fine Mary."

She picked up that flower and fumbled open the

clear plastic, finally lifting the flower out like a new baby. She studied it for what seemed like forever. The rose had probably been at the gas station for quite a while because the edges of the crimson petals were beginning to blacken. Even from arms length she could smell something sweet over the smell of gasoline. Not that she could think about it.

"Honey don't talk nonsense! You deserve flowers; all we girls do." Dannie smiled and winked as if he were letting her in on a secret that he had wanted her to know all along. He steadied his wig, and those bright finger nails flashed in Mary's eyes.

Her face got all solemn and she wondered about Dannie for a moment.

"Why honey underneath this wig there's lots of surprises." Dannie winked at her and began laughing.

Mary who was used to being targeted by laughter, started pushing away, but this was somehow different. Dannie seemed to actually like her…not in any complicated way. As far as Griffin and chicken soup and hairy arms and roses…her body tensed.

The sound of a spatula whacking the grill again rang through the cafe like an alarm. Shirley's dark presence swirled towards Mary.

Dressed in black, like a night that forgot its stars, Shirley sounded like hot, sizzling bacon. "Now Mary, you get back to that kitchen. I'm not paying you to be a hostess. You're a back room girl!"

Mary swallowed her brief moment of introspection and stuffed it way down into her stomach. Her face stiffened into a frightened mask, and her hand squeezed around the rose so tightly that a thorn pierced her thumb. She was beyond sensation now. The sound of the banging spatula echoed through her head, a mistake, a mistake, a mistake. This time she really must have made a terrible mistake, because Shirley's eyes were staring at her ready to pop hot grease at her any moment now. The word "seven" whispered across Mary's mind, and then she contracted, caving into that deep flaw that was herself. Mary turned toward the kitchen, she was even grateful to be reminded to hide herself back there. Slouching away she forgot to say good bye to her friends. After all if they really knew what she was like...

As the swinging door closed off Mary, Dannie looked from Griffin and then to Shirley. "Back room girl my ass!"

Shirley's eyes popped hot grease at Griffin. His toes and fingers and nose and tongue, all his extremities, went limp and cold. Only his eyes could helplessly watch as Shirley branded him and set Mary to flight.

Normally when anyone tried to mold and punish him, he simply scampered away. Not that he was a coward; he just had a fine sense of geographic possibility. Why waste time defending territory when each moment flooded in and barely left him time to remember about what should have been.

But something different was happening; he couldn't scamper away; he'd be leaving Mary to be punished for something that was meant for him. That trail of fineness that she left behind last night tied him to a spot from which, powerless, he couldn't escape. His body shivered in the unusual predicament of staying put.

Shirley shot one last scathing, reproachful look at Griffin and bounded back to the lunch counter. With another smashing bang of her lethal spatula, she cleared the grill.

Tex, a woman of few words, watched. Then she placed her silverware and her napkin on her plate making sure that at least for herself, the mess was taken care of. While Griffin was squirming with a helpless look on his face, and Dannie was muttering something about a hornet stuck in someone's panty hose; Tex mopped her face that always seemed to be damp, looked at Griffin and Shirley with a steady, wide awake look, and finally picked up her check. "See you tomorrow."

Mary stumbled into the kitchen; pressed the magic button. The dish washing machine huffed encouragement, and steam filled the air hiding her from the world. She had work to do: squatting, reaching, pushing, her body melted into movement, and before she knew it, everything outside the kitchen became a dream. While the rotary arm inside the dish washer spun squirting hot water in a reassuring rhythm, life became simple again, at least in the kitchen.

Around 4:30 p.m., Shirley waltzed through the swinging door from her domain in the front room. She had a glittering, sympathetic look on her face, as if she were about to win the Nobel Peace Prize. While Mary opened the dish washer door and steam poured out, Shirley hovered benignly, and for the first time Mary had ever seen, Shirley sat down on a bench in the back room, gracing Mary with a more permanent presence.

The camouflage of the steam allowed Mary to pretend that no one was watching her. She pulled the steaming tray of dishes out, and sprung up holding that hot, dripping tray and placed it on a metal shelf at shoulder level. Then she reached down to the waist high counter and picked up the last tray of dishes. She squatted down and slipped it into the arms of the waiting machine. Sprinkling a little detergent over the tray she closed the door so that the mystery of dish washing could occur. Finally she pressed a button on the machine and it sprung to steamy, shuddering life.

Mary turned around to see tears slipping down Shirley's cheeks. At first Mary thought that Shirley had been slicing onions for the hash browns, but then she noticed an unfamiliar droopy look that made Shirley's vivid penciled eyebrows and coal black hair all the more dramatic. Something was different. As the mascara began smearing down Shirley's cheeks, Mary recognized sadness. Yes it was sadness all right. Mary's whole body heaved, reacting in automatic, wrenching tenderness.

Once upon a time, tenderness had known no name for Mary; it happened as automatically as the seasons, but in these last few months, transplanted from her familiar home, she had begun actually noticing something out of the ordinary. It was like an itch that had to be scratched whenever she saw someone in pain. The more she tried to stop that itching, the more she thought about the person's pain. Finally that accelerating pain pushed her to make some lumbering attempt to make everything better. Though she knew it was happening now, knowing didn't stop her from struggling frantically to save that floundering person in front of her even if Mary's earnestness dragged both of them down. Still...at least that feeling had a name now, "tenderness." For the length of the wash cycle, Mary tenderly sat on the bench next to her glamorous boss.

When the machine finally shuttered and paused between cycles, Shirley leapt up and into motion. As she spoke, her body made solemn dirge like motions, slow and angular. Periodically her arms would thrust open toward Mary as tears lengthened the streaks of mascara on her face. Mary's heart was wrenched with pity.

"Doll, my heart is breaking." Shirley bent forward and went limp, long dark hair hanging forward like a veil of grief. The pain of her shattered heart was too much for even valiant Shirley to stand. "But doll, I need to talk about this."

Bewildered, Mary glanced at Shirley.

Shirley fastened her eyes onto Mary drawing her into the force field of anguish. Mary. "I need to talk with you."

Mary struggled to turn away and then finally heaved a sigh of guilty sympathy.

"I know you didn't mean to betray me, but after all I did for you, you wounded me deeply."

Mary's head began drooping in shame...another terrible mistake.

A look of outrage flashed on Shirley's face.

Even with head down, Mary could feel the piercing heat.

A veil of brittle kindness covered Shirley's face. Her voice which had become shrill, softened. "I know it's not your fault; after all we all know that you're a little slow. I'm very patient with you."

Mary glanced up, relieved. After all everybody knew that she was stupid, yes stupid. Shirley would be patient with her, patient enough to put up with Mary. She nodded gratefully at Shirley.

Like a character out of a Greek tragedy, Shirley began her lamentation. "That pip squeak out there broke my heart!" Her arms thrust upward pleading to the gods for vengeance. "He invited me to his house once too...chicken soup and oh so much kindness. Then on that sofa...we DID IT, Mary; we DID IT! Fickle Griffin won my heart. I know he's not much to look at, but I thought I could make something of him. After all, I've been a dancer in New York."

"I bought him clothes. Somebody had too, Mary; you see how he looks! I enrolled him at a course at the Open University called CALLING FORTH YOUR INNER EXECUTIVE. I knew that I deserved a powerful man, someone who I could look up to. For his birth day, I gave him a certificate to join the gym...I sacrificed so much for that man!"

Mary listened intently her mouth hanging open.

"And what does he do? He gets quieter and quieter. Finally he quits going to class and the gym. When he stopped wearing all those new clothes, I knew he was trifling with my heart." Shirley now pressed her hands to her heart and lowered herself to her knees. A pitiful sob escaped from her lips. "If he really loved me, doll, he would have changed. After all I did for him, he betrayed me. One day when he invited me for supper, as if that could make up for the way he let me down; I decided to confront him: either he snap in line or I leave! And doll, like I said, we had been INTIMATE. Do you catch my drift?"

Even sitting on the bench Mary's body jolted forward. Images of hairy forearms, an arm around her. The sweat stained undershirts of her father spun like a frantic merry go round in her imagination. She was starting to feel dizzy and nauseated.

Though her body was heaving, she focused her attention on helping someone else, yes, Shirley. This person who had practically saved her life by offering her a job was being hurt. This wounded person was looking to Mary for comfort. Her world began to steady. She remembered how Griffin sat sprawled out on the sofa next to her, always pushing a little. He always seemed to want something from her. He did all that and even MORE with Shirley…even more…the dizziness started again. She narrowed her gaze into tunnel vision.

Shirley took on a valiant stance now, her right foot sticking forward, and her left hand holding up some imaginary banner. "I told him to shit or get off the pot and that if I didn't see a change real quick, I would leave him in the pitiable condition I found him. He looked at me in that twitching way of his. Of all the humiliating things, he took off his shoes! I never could stand his toes.

Then he looked at me as if he were innocent and said that he couldn't do what I wanted. His head kept turning from side to side like he was looking for a way out. Without so much as an apology he said that maybe we didn't fit together, and that if I needed to go, I should go; as if I was the one who needed to do something. Here I was being kind enough to help him live up to his potential."

The words now were storming down on Mary, too many words, too many things she didn't want to understand, but she knew Shirley needed her.

A few tears trickled down Shirley's left cheek. "I stormed out of his apartment. I know when somebody is insulting me, doll! I'm a woman of the world." She stuck her chin out defiantly and stood ramrod straight.

Mary's head bobbled in agreement.

"After that he never apologized for not trying harder. I watched him turn back into the mess that he was before I started helping him. At first I thought that he was one of those puny sexless men who can't rise to the occasion of a real woman, but then I saw him ogling you, doll...I finally understood. He's a PREDATOR, out to trifle with feminine hearts and trample them. He even stooped to trifle with you, doll. She reached a protective arm towards Mary.

"I won't let what happened to me, happen to you. After all you're not nearly as capable as I am, and you might get hurt. We'll show him...he can't go around doing those things to us!"

Mary remembered all those dry pot roast dinners that she slowly ate and ate, trying to prevent her mother from being called into the bedroom.

Shirley was resolute now, her arm slicing the air like a protective sword, slashing at the sly cruelty of Griffin.

Now Mary was steaming and trembling like the dish washing machine. The rotary arms of her tenderness were spinning faster and faster, barely interrupting the heated acceleration, Mary heard a little clanging sound, some piece of silverware had slipped down and was hitting the rotary arm without actually stopping its progress. Then, of all the strange things, she thought she smelled oranges. Stupid, stupid Mary!

She sat upright in resolution. She, Mary Blu, NEEDED to save Shirley. "Aw Shirley, he shouldn't have treated you that way; after all you did for him." She stood up reaching her arms toward her vulnerable friend.

Just as Mary was about to stumble into those valiant, wounded arms, Shirley closed her arms. After all Mary was sweating.

Mary froze before those closed arms and realized that she wasn't worthy of this magnificent person. After all, Mary had accepted Griffin's invitation and was responsible for Shirley's pain. Mary tried to make amends. "That Griffin, he shouldn't have done that to you."

Shirley's luxurious sobs began ebbing; a smile spread across her face. "We girls have to stick together. We'll get him. He'll be sorry he treated us that way!"

Mary squirmed under the weight of that smile. She remembered something about seven mistakes a day and the smell of chicken soup. She shook those memories off her. "Well, um, Shirley, I wouldn't want to hurt him, but

I sure won't let him hurt you again. You've been so good to me, giving me a job and all. Loyalty is loyalty."

In an instant Shirley sprang away from Mary and towards the swinging door. Caught in her usual tight velocity she pushed through into the front room. Mary distinctly heard a trailing voice say, "Don't forget doll, loyalty is loyalty."

Chapter 12

The sky to the East was darkening, the air scraped her face with cold; Mary barged down the sidewalk stoking her loyalty. Sometimes she imagined giving eloquent speeches about not hurting people. Sometimes her stiff body would convulse into rage dark and green like stormy sky. Most of all her body ached with guilt at the thought of betraying Shirley. She'd have to make up for that now, she really would. The only thing that she really wanted now was to go to bed; to crawl between her sheets and forget about her life. What was it worth anyway? She always seemed to be betraying people...stupid, stupid Mary. At least this time she'd do it right. She wouldn't let Shirley be hurt.

Her mind filled with pictures, memories. As a child she remembered coming back in the house late on Sunday afternoons after she and Arlene had been sent outside. After the horrible commotion in the bedroom, her father would strut out into the living room, turn the television on and watch the ball game with absolute intensity. He had most of his clothes on except for his shoes, stockings and shirt. She could see that stained undershirt riding up around his hairy belly. That's when her mother would step out of the bedroom, her tight little bun of graying hair lopsided and a look on her face so far away that she couldn't even wave good bye. She'd disappear in the bathroom. For the next hour the sound of toilet flushing and water running, and finally gargling would ring through the house. Her mother would finally step out with another dress on and that bun of hair straight and yanked so tight that her eyes were pulled wide open in a terrible stare. That was the look, that was the look that made Mary want to throw herself at her father screaming.

Eating, she should have kept eating that dried roast beef and scorched mashed potatoes. It was Mary's fault, if only she had tried harder. All the while her father sat there with bare, hairy feet. This time, this time, Mary would save Shirley. She had to this time.

She stumbled home that evening, the darkness gathering. There…she could make out her apartment building drawing near, eventually looming over her; blinding determination moved her forward.

Right in front of her apartment she ran right into a short male silhouette with wild looking hair.

She squinted her eyes and without apologizing stopped and then backed away. It was Griffin. Even in the gloom, she recognized that smile of his that seemed to lead her somewhere that she was afraid to go. His feet were scraping away at the sidewalk, and his shoulders were pressed up towards his ears, as if they were being propped up by some sort of resolve.

For a moment, the smell of wood burning in a stove somewhere in the neighbor woke her to the evening, but then loyalty and something more terrible froze her body again. In that dismal evening, a few feet away from Griffin; her eyes, her whole face assumed their bitter resolve. Something darker than night blinded her.

Maybe it was too dark for Griffin to notice her stony stare. "Mary, there's something I want to talk with you about. You don't have to do anything with it or even answer me, but I want you to know something." He was staggering now as if the sidewalk were shifting underneath him. He kept focusing on Mary's dark shape to catch his balance.

"I've been attracted to women before, but it never really felt right. When I first saw you, there was something different about you. I wanted to know what it would be like to lie in your big arms. Every time you came around; I couldn't take my eyes off you. It took me a month to get up the courage to ask you to supper. And then when you were actually in my apartment, I could hardly believe it, except I could smell you."

In the cover of darkness, Mary's frozen face turned red and and angry.

"You were simply there Mary; you didn't have to do anything, and I didn't have to do anything either. I didn't just smell you Mary, I heard you breathe. I never heard a women breathe before. I was always too busy trying to please them. I don't have to please you Mary; you're just Mary Blu plain and simple."

Mary's silhouette was very, very still for the longest moment that Griffin had ever known. He didn't look from side to side, and his feet were still.

Then like some huge glacier shifting, Mary's voice cracked. "How dare you call me simple! How dare you say I smell! What do you want to do with me, to just to use me, and then make fun of me? I know what you did to Shirley; you used her. You pretend like you care, but I know what you really want me to do!" The memory of hairy toes rumbled through her and crashed on this little man.

She was finally doing it, getting back at the world for all her pain. She stood like a dark sentinel of justice at some final judgment. Her whole body was heaving with a luxurious anger that she had never felt before. She would make that wretch squirm.

Griffin put his hand to his mouth and stared straight out dazed, but even now he didn't try to look for an escape. His dark form stood their, even though his shoulders drooped down under the weight of all that cold rage.

Mary couldn't see how sad his eyes were...she had, she really had to keep her resolve fired.

"You don't need to say anything more Mary. There's so much I want to explain, but I know you can't hear me." He paused for a moment hoping for something, hoping for anything, and then even that escape disappeared. In a whisper he said, "Goodnight now." His little form moved into the darkness.

Chapter 13

That night Mary only ate potato chips, and she hardly noticed the harmonica music next door. She kept running Griffin's villainies over and over in her mind blocking out the sad strains of that nightly music. Despite her vigilance, one plaintive chord snuck through, and she looked out of her kitchen window and wondered why she wanted to hurt him. She quickly covered that up with loyalty and kept eating potato chips, feeling sicker and sicker; her stomach began throbbing; a liquid sour taste began flushing into her mouth. Her whole self began dissolving into a strange and terrible momentum; indignation evaporated into some juicy sour urge.

As her face flushed she rushed to the toilet, lifted the toilet seat resting her arms on the cool white toilet. That gave her just enough relief to lower her head in defeat to convulse and release a sour mass of potato chips into the toilet; the sound throbbing, convulsing in her ears, and resounding in the ceramic bowel around her head.

Her urgency beginning to subside, she experienced a terrible flashing vision…she had hurt somebody, not by accident, but because she wanted to. This time she couldn't even say it was an accident; she had decided, decided to do it. She sat back on her haunches before the white altar of her transgression, replaying the memory of her fatal meeting with Griffin. One minute, she was valiantly protecting Shirley, and the next she'd feel ashamed of trying to hurt someone…somehow images from her past kept mixing in the brew, unbidden: hairy belly, oranges, bare feet, chicken soup,the way hermother looked coming out of the bedroom,the gentle way Griffen had looked at her. Her mind spun and spun on the tiled bathroom floor…no conclusions or insights or any kind of pattern that made sense. Finally in abject defeat she lifted her head, placed her icy disembodied fingers on the metal toilet handle and pressed. She, entranced, watched each disgusting piece of unchewed potato chip spinning round and round, finally reluctantly disappearing into the gurgling hole that seemed to lead to nowhere. If there was a "where," those memories went to…they disappeared into… what or where or how spinning into nothingness. Then even the sound of the gurgling water dissipated into the last strains of the evening music. Then even that stopped.

When Roxanne knocked on the door that night, Mary didn't answer. Images kept swirling around so fast down the drain that she couldn't even focus on the sodden potato chips spinning into oblivion.

Chapter 14

The following day was not a fortunate day for Mary. At the start of her shift, she kept forgetting if she had actually put soap in the dishwasher. She did some loads three or four times. Shirley kept swinging into the back room saying, "We'll show him, doll," and Mary would forget again. In fact around 2 p.m., no matter how many times Shirley had come back to reassure her protégée, those dishes kept piling up in the sink. By 4 p.m., the time that Mary was usually packing up the last tray of dirty dishes into the dish washer, she stood staring blanking at dishes overwhelming the kitchen.

This time when Shirley came back she studied those stacks of dirty dishes ominously. "Hey doll, do you think you're at the beach or something? You got to get moving."

Sure enough, Mary forgot again whether she put detergent into the machine. She ran the load through again for the seventh time.

5 p.m., Shirley came back one last time. She stared at

those dishes while tapping her right foot. "You gotta be kidding! Well doll I have things to do tonight. You can lock up. You oughta be able to manage that."

At 8:00 p.m., Mary limped out of Surely's front door; she walked, downtrodden, so much like those many times she returned to the house on the dead end street that was a graveyard for any hopes. Back then, walking home after her night shift at the nursing home, all she could really ask for was that whatever mistake she made would be forgotten so that she could keep up this futile grind without slipping into some terrifying abyss: her own private terror with no name.

Her hand fumbled in her pocket searching for the keys, wondering if she could actually unlock the door to her building. Her honeymoon with dish washing, like her first honeymoon with The Rainbow was disintegrating in the storm of her anguish.

She started wondering what she'd do next now that she had failed at this job. That's when she noticed a dark, angry little form waiting for her by the front stoop of her apartment. It was too dark for Mary to notice that "MARY BUTCHUNK, MARY BUTCHUNK, MARY BUTCHUNK" was written in red letters up and down the sidewalk.

When Roxanne saw Mary's shadowy form walk up that sidewalk, Roxanne heaved a big sigh and her anger started melting into relief. She was actually glad that Mary couldn't see the writing on the sidewalk. Besides Roxanne was already fighting with everybody else in her life, and if she lost Mary...Roxanne couldn't think about that. After all Mary had become a part of her life, just like that pink barrette she stuck in her hair every morning even when unhappiness seemed to stretch on forever. Besides Roxanne really wanted to learn how to braid.

"Where were you last night Mary, where were you? You promised me you'd show me how to braid. You broke your promise." Mary's big clumsy body cringed at the sight of that frantic, threatening girl, and something hid deeper inside Mary. She didn't bother to stoop down to Roxanne's level; Mary was too tired for that. "Braiding, oh, the braiding." Mary's eyes squinted and she surged with prickly embarrassment as she realized that she had just betrayed someone else.

Those two stood there motionless shadows. Though Mary's mind was as dark as the evening had become, Roxanne could still focus on some kind of personal need, a hazy form of hope.

For the last two weeks Roxanne had watched that heap of rags in Mary's apartment turn into what looked like piles and piles of colored ribbons. In those first two weeks of school, thinking about those ribbons helped Roxanne get by. No matter how bad school was she could look forward to herself and Mary turning those ribbons into braids, wonderful braids.

She didn't like school much, not at all. If anyone asked her about school, she would simply drop her head and glance from side to side before turning into stone. This was a good enough answer for most adults who long ago had mastered the skill of turning to stone themselves. But if you pressed Roxanne, asking and cornering her, that dull evasive face would become animated with fury, a different daimon held sway, a louder banging daimon that didn't understand sadness anymore, just revenge.

During class she had to sit in a desk, stared at by a teacher who expected to her to remember all sorts of things that Roxanne had never learned. Time between classes was even worse; she didn't even have the safety of her desk. She had to try to squeeze into the wiggling mass of her classmates and pretend that she belonged. She wasn't good at pretending, and her classmates always seemed to smell her out and in no uncertain terms let her know that, especially with that dumb old pink barrette. Roxanne learned to master the skill of not making eye contact with anyone during the course of a day. Once when two boys cornered her in the lunch room and tried to yank that old barrette out of her hair, she bit them. People learned to keep a wide birth around her. Even teachers became frightened at the threatening look on her face when they pressed to hard for an answer. Broken promise or not, Roxanne was glad to see Mary.

"Come on Mary we got braids to do. You promised."

Mary's head bobbled in an automatic nod. She fiddled with the key and door knob for a few minutes, forgot to check the mail, and plodded up the stairs with Roxanne in tow. After a few desperate moments during which Mary thought that she would never get into her apartment door she chanced upon the right combination of turning the key and the doorknob. Mary flicked the light switch on; the two stepped into the apartment.

Mary spoke like a wooden puppet. "Do you want some

coolaid Roxanne?" Without waiting for an answer, Mary mechanically walked into the kitchen to get it.

After all the waiting, the pile of ribbons now looked more like cut up old rags to Roxanne. She was just about to harden up her fists and beat the air again when she heard Mary drop a glass. Even though it was plastic and kind of bounced on the floor, Roxanne began wondering. After all Mary was the most beautiful, graceful person she had ever known. Angry disappointment turned into something else softer. "Are you sick Mary, I mean really sick?"

As Mary mechanically filled the glasses with coolaid, she heard the word "Mary" and then the word "sick" and for the first time in twenty four hours realized that she didn't feel well. She stood silently by those two glasses of liquid that sparkled red through the scratched plastic and all the memories of the last two days started revolving again around that feeling of being sick; no it wasn't exactly sick. That was last night. For the first time that evening she noticed harmonica music. It seemed, well it seemed so sad.

Yes, that's what she was feeling, sad, so sad. Quite suddenly she felt the ground beneath her feet. It's like she was slow dancing to that sadness in the air. Her face began to soften.

She walked back into the living room. "I threw up last night. I heard you knock. I couldn't get up. I didn't feel so good."

That talk about throwing up was a reassuring revelation to Roxanne. She began bouncing up and down. "Boy, throwing up, I know what that's like. Once I threw up in bed. I woke up and there was throw-up all over me, and I was crying. I didn't know what to do, and then I fell back asleep. When I woke up, I even washed my face, but everybody in school said I smelled. They'd hold their noses when I walked by. My teacher even sent me home with a note. I didn't let my mother see it."

Maybe it was the memory of the smell of throw-up, but Mary looked like she was coming alive. She could see Roxanne smelling all sour while other children held their noses. "Didn't your mother help you clean up?"

Roxanne generally didn't like questions, but after all, Mary didn't feel good, and Roxanne was more than familiar with that state of being. Most adults tried to look happy, or if they couldn't do that they usually found someone to blame, especially Roxanne. Mary plain and simple just didn't feel good. Roxanne bent over toward Mary as if she were telling a secret. There were some things that she had been thinking about. "Mommie doesn't do very much since daddy's testicle became a grapefruit."

Even Mary was stunned.

With the nonchalance of a weather reporter, Roxanne continued. "First daddy started staying in bed a lot. My mother cooked every good thing that she knew how to make, but he still wouldn't get out of bed. That's when I heard her say to daddy in the bedroom, 'Your testicles are so big. You have to see a doctor, Roy. You got grapefruit down there.' I already knew what a testicle was, one of those things that boys have between their legs that makes hair grow on their faces. I know what a grapefruit is. I didn't know that testicles turned into grapefruit sometimes. A few weeks later he went to the hospital and they cut the grapefruit off. But it was too late. You know when a testicle turns into a grapefruit, you die. I'm sure glad I don't have testicles. I'd always be worried it would turn into a grapefruit." Roxanne nodded very solemnly.

Mary's eyes kept getting bigger and bigger until there was so much white around them that it looked like there was a snowstorm inside her head. It wasn't just that she had never heard an eight year old girl talk about testicles; it was understanding that strange and horrible things happen to other people too, not just her. What happened if Dannie got a grapefruit down their or even Griffin? Griffin...for a second she could smell oranges; and she could just see the delicate way his thumbs moved inside the cleft of the orange and with extraordinary tenderness and determination opened it's fleshy petals, as if all along the orange was waiting to spread wide. She mustn't think about that after all he said she smelled.

Mary handed Roxanne a glass of coolaid, and both of them sat on the floor on either side of the heap of cut up rags. "I used to braid Arlene's hair. It was shiny and the color of honey. One whole summer I braided it for her. All the while her hair got lighter and lighter because she was out in the flower garden so much. At first when she asked me to do it, I didn't think I could. I have a hard time with things like that where I have to tell right from left. But then Arlene said I didn't have to know about that. All I had to do was stand behind her and divide her hair back there in to three piles. Even I could see that one of the piles was in the middle." Mary laid out three long strands of rags. One rag was cut from her mother's favorite blue dress. And other was cut from a faded, green plaid bathrobe of her father. The third was cut from a thin, yellow baby blanket on which the name "Mary" was embroidered. Mary laid the yellow strip between the green and the blue.

Roxanne bent over and examined the three strips lying side by side.

"Now Arlene said I didn't have to know which strand was right or left, but just see which one is in the middle. There, do you see that the yellow one is in the middle?"

Roxanne nodded while she kept her eyes glued to those colored strips. For once her mind didn't wander into all kinds of fidgety directions. She wanted to understand.

"Now Arlene said that it didn't matter which side I started on. I just pick one from the side and cross it over the center strip." She crossed the green plain strip over the yellow strip. "Now here's where the magic starts, Roxanne. Do you see now that the green strip is in the middle?"

Roxanne's eyes opened up in surprise, careful not to look away from the colored strips.

"Then Arlene said to take the strip from the other side. Here this blue one, and cross it over the center again." She crossed the blue material over the green material. "Then you go to the other side. That's yellow now, and you cross that over the middle which is blue now."

And there right before Roxanne's eyes those raggedy strips of yellow blue and green turned into a beautiful braid in which yellow and blue and green seemed to dance, crisscrossing each other in Technicolor. Each time Mary crossed the side strip over the middle strip the beautiful braid grew like it was alive.

"Come on Mary let me do it, come on it's my turn Mary. Show me. Show me."

"All right Roxanne. Sit here right next to me. Okay now. Last time I crossed the strip on this side over the middle, so now, Roxanne, cross the strip on the other side over the middle.

Roxanne did. "What if it doesn't work Mary?"

"I'll help you for a while Roxanne. It'll work. Now take the strip on the other side of the middle one and cross it over. There that's it."

The Technicolored braid began growing again. "Mary, look Mary, I'm braiding. I'm braiding." Roxanne's whole body was bouncing up and down as she stared at those strips of color and kept crossing them over each other just like Mary said. Then Roxanne began crossing them over each other even before Mary told her. In a tour de force that absolutely amazed Mary, Roxanne began saying, "Now I'll put the right one over the middle; and now, the left one over the middle." Roxanne was very smart. Her eyes and hands and lips and brains worked all together.

Mary noticed that the green strip was getting dangerously short. She reached her hand in the pile and pulled out a black strip from her father's old suite and she laid the end of it over the shortening green end; without skipping a beat Roxanne began weaving black in the braid instead of green. Both of the friends were surprised to see that the braid was still beautiful, just different. Then Mary grabbed a white strip from Arlene's first communion dress and placed it on the blue strip that was running out. The braid was black and yellow and white now.

For hours they both stared at the lengthening, color changing braid; Roxanne hands flying from side to side and, Mary kept pulling out strips of color from her pile of memories. They braided for hours; Mary even forgot to eat supper. Magic caught them both up. Roxanne was getting so good at braiding that her hands kept accurately moving while she looked up at Mary. "Mary, do you think I could bring one of my raggedy dresses and we could turn that into a braid too, just like with your sister Arlene's dress?"

Mary was so amazed at Roxanne's feat of skill that she nodded. Yes, two people could do something together.... amazing!

The pile of rags was disappearing; not exactly disappearing, but becoming something else.

"Roxanne, look it's 11 p.m. What's your mother going to say? You better go home!"

"It doesn't matter Mary. I stay up as late as I want. Besides my mother met this new man who lives in Milwaukee. She's real busy with him. I sure hope his testicles turns into a grapefruit."

Chapter 15

As soon as Mary woke up to the sound of whirring tires outside, she jumped out of bed. The cold floor tickled her feet; she tiptoed into the living room. There, long and coiled and ever changing lay the braid magically transforming into a rug. She and Roxanne had done that; it wasn't a dream. Solemnly Mary walked over to the rug, and sitting down laid it across her lap. Eyes closed, she caressed the knobby firm length of it. Funny all her memories had turned to this.

Her eyelids pushed closed, as she remembered newer memories, Griffin and Shirley and work. Her hands stopped their luxurious caressing and blood began pounding through her head. Why did she have to be so mean to Griffin?

She pushed the coil aside and began dressing urgently, occasionally snorting in rough little bursts of air when she remembered the mess in which she found herself. Indeed, she knew she was in the middle of it. Every move she made, she hurt somebody. First she hurt Shirley without knowing it, and then she hurt Griffin...she wanted to hurt him. Her whole life she had maneuvered desperately trying not to hurt people. And whenever she was hurt, well that wasn't so bad, because after all she was stupid, and stupid people get hurt. This time was different; Mary knew she had tried to hurt; maybe, just maybe she even enjoyed it.

Mary walked to work slowly that morning as if she were picking her way through a mine field, moving through the cool air that was shaking leaves loose. She stepped into the sizzling air of Surely's. Her necked drooped on its delicate stem in a gesture of extravagant submission. On her scissors hand side, she heard the whacking of Shirley's spatula...her right. She peaked over to her rag holding side...her left. Dannie and Tex waved like this was any other morning. Griffin was there too, but he didn't look up. He sat hunched in his chair staring at plateful of food.

"Hey doll, grab that cart and get started. We don't want to repeat yesterday do we?" Mary peaked at her right and grabbed the cart. She was just about to flee into the kitchen, when she felt something delicately touch her shoulder, like one of those falling leaves outside. She turned. There stood Griffin, except he wasn't looking at her. Though his whole body was limp, he stood there steady. Only those long hairs coming out of his brow quivered and betrayed his agitation. "I'm sorry if I scared you." Then he took one quick look at Mary, "it's not what your thinking...no excuse...it's just not that...omly best wishes to you." before Mary could even think about what was happening, he turned and went back to the table.

She tried to hang her head low enough to slip away and escape into the vague never land of confusion: once again any hopes or plans lay in tatters encircling her. Then, in all that messines she smelled the coffee and bacon pulling her from the inside and outside back to the morning in Surely's Cafe. She made a jangly but determined exodus into the backroom, leaving the door to the kitchen swinging.

She heard the door flapping again and again behind her like an accusation, "stupid, stupid, stupid," but with each swinging flap she noticed the sound of "stupid" diminishing until it was a whisper and then quiet. She stood still for a moment, listening to the silence, and then walked over and touched the steaming, quivering dish washer for consolation. Yes, she had work to do. As far as messiness, well, there was no escape.

Almost on its own she began lifting and stretching in a graceful economy of motion. The dish washer huffed, its rotary arm spinning reassuringly, and the dirty dishes disappeared to become clean dishes.

Ten minutes later Shirley swirled into the kitchen. "Hey doll, was he bothering you?"

Mary looked up out of the steam for a moment and then kept working. It's not that she was being defiant, she simply didn't know what to think, let alone say.

"You gotta watch out for him; he's tricky." She fastened her gaze on Mary. "What did he say. What did he say; tell me."

Mary looked down at her hands. They were wet and soapy. She glanced at Shrley and shook her head ever so slightly. Yes, as far as messiness there was no escape. She grabbed another tray of dirty dishes.

"Well if you want to be that way about it, doll..." Shirley's face became hard as a stone as she smashed through the swinging door.

Mary shook her head for a moment. She knew nothing she could do would make things better. She lid the tray of dirty dishes into the dish washer and nodded softly; she could do right by this job, even if she was about to loose it. She spent the rest of the day doing dishes very well, and almost forgot about the front room.

4:30 p.m. Mary was squirting water into the sinks, rinsing them out. The steam in the kitchen was beginning to disappear. Like her mother long ago, Mary began dragging out this time in the kitchen before she had to face the rest of her life. Finally there were no tasks left to be done. She pulled her hair net off, hung it on a nail and slipped through the swinging door. She grabbed her pile of tips and squeaked out a goodbye. Shirley stared at her and blew smoke from her funneled lips. "You gotta be kidding."

Mary made it to the outside. The air was cool, crackling with the sound of leaves under her feet. Just as she began sinking into guilt about her own mistakes, a cool end-of-summer breeze brushed through her clothes and tickled her sweaty body. She paused for a moment there on the sidewalk feeling the inner tickle mixing with the sounds of a Minneaplois afternoon in fall. Once again her feet started moving on the sidewalk, she remembered the braid and began kicking through the leaves as she walked home, yes, home.

Funny, Roxanne wasn't there waiting for her. She did notice an envelope taped to her door. On it was a name: "Mary Blue" written in blue ink. She slipped it into a pocket of her dungarees. After all she had made so many mistakes in the last couple of days that one more hardly mattered. She nodded softly...mistakes, mistakes; the world is filled with mistakes.

That evening Mary hardly fumbled with the keys at all. She stepped into her apartment as the windows caught the last rays of day and then sat down next to the spiralling braid. She opened the envelope and then the sheets of paper within it; the crackling sound mixed with the sound of blowing leaves from that old cottenwood tree outside the window. For some reason she thought of Ariadne. The name "Griffin" was signed at the end of the note.

She sighed. Was it relief, guilt or just confusion? Things were mixing up in a strange sort of way.

Dear Mary Blu,

When I was ten I was riding my bike through a path in the woods on a beautiful sunny morning. Things couldn't have been better. Summer seemed like forever. That's when I hit a patch of sand, and my bike tipped over to the side with me on it. I fell right into a bush. That normally wouldn't have been so bad, but there was a hornets' nest in it. They started buzzing and stinging me. I remember screaming. I jumped up as fast as I could and started running, just running. At first the hornets kept buzzing and stinging me, and then the hornets stopped biting and just buzzed around my head. And then the buzzing stopped and all I heard was my breath pushing in and out all rough and desperate. After a while I stopped running. When I got home, I told my parents that some bigger boys had stolen my bike. I was afraid they'd send me back to get it if I told them what happened.

I never did have a bike after that, and I never went back to that place in the woods ever again. I don't know if this makes any sense to you, Mary, but when I met you Friday night, I felt like I had stumbled into a hornets' nest. I got away from you quickly, but this time, I want to come back for the bike. I like you Mary, and even though I know you can't love me, I want to be your friend. That's important to me, so important that I'm writing this letter.

I'm sorry that I upset you. Though the expression of my regard for you may have seemed abrupt, it was never the less real. I won't bother you about those feelings in the future. I wouldn't want to be the cause of pain. There are some things I need to say though.

I can understand how you would feel abhorrence for my behavior with Shirley, but you have only heard her side of that story. I am not ashamed of my behavior towards her, I am only sorry that now I have to disclose things that may discomfort and confuse you.

Shirley and I dated for a couple a year ago. The word dating sounds so strange. I picture teenagers going to movies wondering if it's time to go steady yet. But none of us are teenagers, Mary. I would much rather say that Shirley and I were becoming friends. I invited Shirley to my apartment a couple of times and she invited me to hers. I was attracted to her. I thought she was attracted to me or at least liked me a little. And yes we made love Mary; I don't regret that. Shirley and I had a few moments together that were wonderful for me, and I hope for her too.

Wonderful wasn't enough for Shirley. She started to try to dress me up and tell me how to act with people. She even wanted me to make more money. It wasn't her wanting those things that bothered; it was that she wanted me to want those things as desperately as she did.

I tried but I couldn't. What kind of shoes I wear, and what kind of job I have aren't very important to me. I like things that are simpler: sunny mornings, a friend's smile, making chicken soup with fresh rosemary, playing my harmonica in the evening, oranges...those kind of things, Mary. Maybe someday when I'm old and poor (the old part isn't so very far away and the poor part is already here), I may regret the life that I've lived.

Still, all and all Mary, I don't want to stop living today to get myself ready for a future that I fear. I don't know why I'm telling this to you Mary, but something about you I trust. Whether you're spilling milk, or talking to that little girl, or even being mad at me; I know somebody is in their working real hard. I respect that person Mary, and I'll always give you at least seven mistakes a day.

I know I'm getting off the point here, but all this stuff is connected. When I finally told her that I needed to stop trying to be the person I thought she wanted me to be, I hoped that she would see me as I am, and maybe like me. I hardly expect to be loved by a woman.

She got more angry than I ever saw her before. More angry than when I didn't want to get fancy running shoes, more angry than when I said that I didn't want to go to school to become a business executive, even more angry than when I got uncomfortable wearing those skimpy bright colored underwear that she bought for me.

When it seemed to finally sink in on her that she couldn't change me into the person that she wanted me to be; her face became hard and cold as a brick wall in winter. When she threatened to go, I just let her go. She seemed pretty unhappy with me, not just once and a while, but regularly.

I miss her, the way she laughs and dances; but I got tired trying to be someone that I'm not. I thought that things would eventually be all right between us, like two old friends; and for a while I thought things were.

Then you came along Mary; I wasn't looking for someone, but there you were. I hoped that you might care about me. I know I don't have much to offer, and if that was the reason you wouldn't have wanted me, I would have understood that. I knew though that you're being angry with me was based at least partially on what you had heard from Shirley. I want you to know that what happened between Shirley and I was very complex, at least more complex than one person's point of view.

So here, this letter is my point of view. I have regard for you Mary, and I'll leave you free to come to any conclusions that you need to make.

I know how you like Tex. Normally she doesn't interfere in other people's business, but if you need to talk with someone about things, she would be a good person. You see she is friends with both Shirley and I.

Again, I apologize for my precipitous declaration and the difficulty it caused you. I won't disrupt your life like that in the future. I hope that once again you may join us at the breakfast table and know that I feel only consideration and respect for you.

Your Friend, I hope,
Griffin Frank

Mary sat on the floor with the letter lying open on her lap wondering why she felt so sad that Griffin wouldn't disrupt her life again in the future. The sun dipped behind the building across the street; she felt a shiver of cold. Someone had actually been in love with her, or pretty close to it. Somehow she had missed it all. Of course it was too late now, especially if Griffin was telling the truth. But why would he say that she could talk to Tex, if he wasn't telling the truth? If Griffin was ashamed or lying, wouldn't he want to hide? Her mind kept picking at the knot. What if she had not only been mean but stupid...stupid Mary. Why would anyone want to be around her, let alone love her? How could she ever expect him to love her after the way she treated him. He saw her stupid meanness; she's lucky he still wants to be a friend.

Her hand dropped to the braid coiled beside her, the harmonica music had started again. She sat still listening for a moment, and then stood up in the gloom and turned the lights on. She had supper to make, and even more exciting tonight was the night she was going to begin sewing that braid into the ever widening circles of her rug. A chord of music tickled her deep in her stomach. Of course it was too late now for Griffin to love her, especially if he was telling the truth.

She walked over to the kitchen table and picked up the box with needles and threads in it. She studied those sewing supplies with absolute attention and carefully lifted out a very big needle and a spool of very thick, black thread.

She sat down once again by the coiling braid, took in

a deep breath, held it for a moment of absolute calmness, and then released it in a long sigh that she didn't push out; she simply let it go. Then, after a moment of stillness, she took the end of the braid and curved it into the very first tiny circle.

Right before she crawled under her covers very late that night, she wondered where Roxanne was.

Chapter 16

T hat night, she jerked herself awake in a heart pumping start, trying to prevent herself from falling. She jumped out of bed, ran in to the bathroom and released a torrent of pee…harmonica, Griffin…what if…she flushed with guilt. She had experienced guilt before when she made a mistake, but this was different; she couldn't just try to forget about it and hope that she wouldn't be caught. This time she had actually stepped into the situation. Sitting in darkness on the cold toilet seat, her body relaxed. She walked into the living room, turned on the light, and saw that it was only 4:00 AM…two more hours to sleep. She walked over to the small circle that she had created in the evening, a snail shell of a spiral.

Without thinking, she grabbed for the needle and thread, and before her very eyes that spiral started growing. The colors didn't just dance up and down the braid, but now they pulsed through the whole growing shell. Who would have thought that old, disappointing rags could become something so beautiful and alive?

At 6 a.m. the last thing that she remembered before nodding off was the smell of oranges. Her alarm went of at 6:30. At first she felt embarrassed for staying up at night, but as she stared down at that ever growing spiral, she felt proud about her daring. She pulled on a Star Trek tee shirt, slipped into a pair of her father's dungarees, smelled yesterday's socks before putting them back on, slipped into nursing loafers, grabbed a jacket, and stepped out of her apartment. She didn't even brush her teeth; that's how daring she was this morning.

The curled leaves outside were coated with milky frost, and a puddle by the curb was glassed over. A crow startled the blue over Mary's head. She walked to work, not serene exactly, but at least all in one piece even with the mistakes, yes walking, cool air, sun, stepping with a certain grace. How very strange.

She opened the door of Surely's and walked into a world that seemed back to normal. Shirley was whacking a pile of potatoes with her spatula and said, "Hi ya doll." Mr. Dannie was straightening his wig in the mirror. Tex was sweating. Griffin looked up at her and smiled. She smiled back, after all what had she to loose?

She walked back to the kitchen without stumbling over anything. That morning as she started her dishes, her day seemed as clear as the blue outside. For a moment Mary wondered if this was the way people felt when they died.

At 9 a.m. she stepped out into the front to pull back

another cart of dishes. Tex was still at the table, wiping her face with a red plaid handkerchief and reading a book. Griffin and Dannie has alrewady left. With nothing to loose anymore, Mary walked over with casual familiarity. "Good morning Tex, how are ya doing?"

Tex looked up, not surprised at all, closed her book entitled ZEN AND THE ART OF MOTORCYCLE MAINTENANCE, and said, "I'm glad to see you this morning." She motioned to the empty chair by the table.

As if being punished for undue familiarity Mary looked down. Her lips squeaked out an answer. "I'd really like to Tex, but you know I have all this work to do, and besides Shirley doesn't like it when I spend too much time out here." All the while Mary's body all on its own was edging toward the table.

Tex looked up. "Hey Shirley, Mary's going to take a break." Shirley looked up from the grill, blew out smoke in the general direction of Mary and Tex. "It's a free country."

Mary accepted her fate and pulled out a chair.

"You're doing fine back there, but you never seem to take a breather. Sit with me a spell."

And Mary did. Now that she knew someone really wanted her there, she calmly sat down.

Tex was a story teller; she put her hands on her haunches and hunkered down. "I stopped trying so darn hard to get people to like me about the time I decided to change my name from Tina to Tex. I wanted to call myself something that had a lot of wide open spaces in it. You know how it is when you need breathing room."

Mary nodded, not with immediate understanding,

because after all she knew so little, but sometimes her innocence made room for almost anything. "Ya, Texas is supposed to be a pretty big place."

"I was Tina from Cleveland for my first twenty five years, but the name was always too small for me. Besides, my parents were always dressing me in pink. Pink gets dirty pretty fast when you're your more interested in crawling under cars to see how they work. When I got a little older and I got my period, my breasts started to stick out and boys stared at them while their eyes popped out. Then they'd nudge each other with shit eating grins. Seems they never looked me in the eye anymore. And girls got pretty strange too. They stopped doing normal things like catching frogs and began wearing real tight clothes that crimped them all up. They even started to walk different, and talked about boys all the time, as if boys was something dreamy and wonderful. Don't get me wrong Mary, men are okay but they're not larger than life, sometimes they're down right delicate. I never understood what all the fuss was about.

Mary shook her head and then her mouth dropped open.

"I heard you got some man trouble. Griffin mentioned that you might be talking to me."

At the mention of Griffin, Mary's head bobbled in embarrassment.

"Normally I keep out of other people's trouble. The way I see it, people spend too much time thinking about what they think should be there and don't notice whats going on." She burst out laughing as if that was the funniest thing imagineable.

Mary watched in bewilderment, but her head tilted slightly towards Tex. She made eye contact with Tex. Her face relaxed into curiosity.

Tex caught the interest. "It seems to me that you're caught in a stampede right now, and I'll pull you up for a ride, so you can find your bearing. After that I'll leave it up to you." Tex placed her hand on Mary's elbow like she was actually going to pull her up from all the man havoc.

Mary nodded almost in spite of herself. That touch steadied her; the head bobbing stopped. She looked straight on at Tex.

"Now I like Griffin. He's my friend, and a good friend he is. I like the way he sees things in a different kind of way. He's life size. Now Shirley's my friend too. Underneath all that cantankerous attitude lies some kind of tenderness trying to break out into the open. She struggles so hard that she can be downright mean sometimes. That's just the way things are for her. She needed Griffen to be something different than who he is, and hasn't figured out that most of what we need comes from the inside.

"Now the stories not finished for Shirley, and I'm going to stick around. But there's no need to get caught in her commotion. Sometimes when things get complicated, all you need to do is take a pee."

A constricting band around Mary's chest loosened; a breath filled her body. Her eyes had a look, not glazed over and not pinched with intensity, but just wide open. She remembered Ariadne from back at The Rainbow, not so much a memory but a melody, happy and sad all mixed up into tenderness.

"Heck, Griffin's a pretty good old range rider. At night when he play's that harmonica of his, you know there's music there."

At the word "harmonica" Mary's eyebrows and shoulders gave a little jerk. "Is he the one who plays the music in the evening?"

"That's him all right."

Now Mary didn't exactly understand everything Tex was saying; the sound of a stampede still echoed through her ears, but the feeling of those soft evening harmonica melodies echoed through her too...yes it was Griffin all the time. Just as she was about to actually say Griffin's name, the door to Surely's swung open and a small desperate face topped with greasy hair and a pink barrette pushed through.

"Mary!" She took a desperate ragged breath. "Mary I was looking for you all over. I thought maybe you'd be here." Roxanne's usually stony suspicion was replaced by a wilder look. "When I got home Thursday real late after helping you with that braid, mom was all angry and worried. You know since my dad's you-know-what turned into a grapefruit, she hasn't worried about me at all." The flood of words paused for a moment while she took choppy little breaths all the time looking straight at Mary. "We went to Milwaukee to see her dumb boyfriend... and I just got back and MARY, mom's going to move us out there. I don't want to go, I don't want to go! I finally have a friend and there's that rug we need to make, and my mom is taking me away Friday after school, and I'll never see you again, and Mary you got to help me!" Her eyes were open wide in a pleading panting stare fixed right on Mary.

Tex wiped her face with her handkerchief and watched.

Mary was staring directly at Roxanne, eyes wide open and panting too. She started rocking in her chair like she was chained to it and wanted to get up but couldn't. She struggled, all caught up and straining. She had to, she had to, she had to save Roxanne, and still she remained fastened to that chair feeling more frantic by the moment, and she couldn't do anything.

Tex looked back and forth from Roxanne's frenzied need to Mary's straining immobility. Tex finally fixed her eyes on Mary's bulging eyes. Mary's helplessness subsided a little. She stopped the rocking, pushed her chair back and stood up. She couldn't walk, because she would have tripped, but she felt the flush of a little something pop inside, and before she could think about it her arms opened up big and strong. The sight of those wide open arms pulled Roxanne in like some huge irresistible magnet and drew her into its embrace. Before either Mary or Roxanne knew what was happening they were caught up together, hearts pumping, breath heaving, and long stored up tears dribbling down their faces. For moments that seemed like forever, Mary's arms wrapped around Roxanne as their heaving breaths.

Finally a big sigh that turned into a yawn came up all the way up from Mary's belly.

Roxanne started squirming. "Mary, what are you going to do Mary, can I live with you?"

Mary's body tightened into a hardly perceptible rocking motion again. Finally she looked down at her friend. "I have to think about this, Roxanne. I don't want to make promises that don't mean anything. Come see me after work. We can work on the rug…I need to spend some time figuring things out."

Roxanne started looking stony, glancing at Mary suspiciously, her face getting angrier by the moment. Finally Roxanne turned to flee.

In a deep voice, not an angry voice either…just very definite, Mary said. "Please come and see me after work. I want to be with you."

Roxanne looked bewildered for an instant and then nodded reluctantly. She didn't slam the door behind her.

Chapter 17

Late that same afternoon, from the window of his apartment, Griffin watched the two walk home, Mary with long steady strides, and Roxanne who skipped and ran to keep up, all the while talking a mile a minute. Just as they disappeared into the big old house, he smiled. Being with women had always been so confusing; he needed to scamper around them to try to please them or to prevent their wrath. In fact he would get so caught up in the scampering that he didn't know anymore why he kept trying so hard let alone if he actually liked it.

But he couldn't help but smile at the memory of Mary Blu. No one could take that away from him, not even Mary. That's when he decided to make chicken soup. After all he liked chicken soup.

Of course it put him a little behind time. Usually like instinctive clock work, he ate supper and then picked up his harmonica. This evening, he sauteed the onions and garlic and celery, browned the chicken, poured in water, and put a few little branches of fresh rosemary. He covered the pot and turned the gas on, and then picked up his instrument. While he sniffed fragrant smells, and his hands cradled the harmonica; he could feel Mary next door. The lights began turning on in the night. He finally ate after he completed his nightly responsibility.

Chapter 18

"That's beautiful Mary, the way you sewed the braid like that all going in a circle. When I live here with you, we can finish it together. I'll be a big help to you Mary." Roxanne was nodding her head up and down so hard that her pink barrette was bouncing on her forehead.

Mary fled to the kitchen saying, "I'll get some coolaid Roxanne."

Roxanne barrette settled down, ominously. With eyes beginning to pinch in suspicion she watched Mary leave. After all Roxanne was a professional at being abandoned. Her voice started taking on a whining sound. "When I live here Mary everything is going to be all right. Isn't it Mary, Mary! Mary I can stay here Mary, I have too." The whining tone started turning into a banging threat. "You're supposed to make everything better. You have to, Mary!"

Mary walked back into the living room holding two

glasses of coolaid. She almost tripped on a leg of the table. "Do you like what I've done on the rug so far, Roxanne?"

"I'm gonna stay here Mary!" Her hands were clumped into fists her arms were shaking. She threw a fast, hard glance at Mary.

Mary's head dropped as if ducking that projectile, then it began bobbling. A very tiny voice came out of her big body. "You see Roxanne it's this way, I really like you and I want you around, but I just can't. You know I really want to, but I just can't. You have your own mother. You really do." Her voice trailed off in supplication.

As Mary's body was turning into a wobbly mass, Roxanne's was hardening. She knew all about adults and how they lied. Little tremors began cracking her rigid little body. "You lied Mary, you lied, you're not my friend! I hate you Mary, I hate you! I hate you! I hate you!"

Mary was too busy ducking to stop Roxanne from running out of the apartment. Only the slamming door startled her enough to stop her bouncing head. She stood there frozen.

Stupid, stupid Mary. Just as it seemed that she would never move again, the sound of the harmonica began winding its way into her tensed body. Yes, she was feeling hurt and angry and frightened and sad all turning into each other like the melody running through her. She stood in that swirl of emotion, her body still…just breathing.

And strangely enough…nothing happened. She didn't explode into disgusting little pieces all over the room. There she was just standing…maybe wiggling her toes a little. Finally, some heavy pressure that had been squeezing her in, began lifting; her body settled into a soft sadness, tenderness that harmonized with the music. She was glad he was next door still playing. It somehow made it easier to stand there and let the feelings swirl into who knows where.

Chapter 19

Mary woke up that night; an icy breeze pushing through the slightly open bedroom window, and with it came the sound of a dog howling in the night. She woke up to the repeating, deep down melody of loss that set the whole dark night filling her chest with grief. As she opened her eyes that rumbling base sound slid up to a high pitched whine that pleaded for something it knew it could never get. While that forlorn melody repeated again, she pulled the covers up around her shoulders to close the chill out. The cry outside stopped; that's when she noticed her toes were cold. The penetrating cold was licking them. She pulled her knees up to her chest to escape the cold tongue; that didn't work. A cold tremor running through her body released a little grunt into the stillness of the room. While the springs of the bed creaked a complaint, she sat up and bent down to the icy floor to feel around in the dark for her socks...there they were. She pulled them on with a slow released sigh, and tilting back into bed, slipped her feet under the covers. That was better; her feet were already heating up. That little shiver was turning into deep-down-under-the-covers warmth. Just before she slid back into her private night she realized that a whole bunch of people were mad or disappointed with her, and still it felt good slipping down into warm ease, letting go. She sank down into sleep.

She found herself in a city. The houses were old and each one had a special garden. Some gardens were filled with red roses and yellow nasturtiums, some were filled with white daisies and purple lilacs. Each yard was filled with different colors and kinds of plants. Whichever way she looked, each yard seemed the most beautiful. Then she passed by a house that she just knew was Roxanne's; the yard was filled with pink flowering crab trees, and every time the wind sighed through them, petals like blushing snowflakes dropped down. Some even fluttered and rested on Mary's head. That's when she noticed the brambles growing there; thorns sharp as needles reached through the pale blossoms ready to snap and tear at anyone nearby, especially little girls with pink barrettes. Mary knew she needed to do something; she didn't want anything to sting Roxanne. With hands strengthened and toughened by dish washing Mary pulled up the brambles out of the ground and tossed them down a deep and dark ravine. She was brushing her hands off feeling mighty proud of herself when the same soft wind that carried pink petals whispered in her ear. "Mary, Mary what are you doing to the garden? Mary, Mary, what are you doing to the garden?" From all the city's gardens now the wind whispered, "Mary, Mary what are you doing to the garden?" That whispering breeze brushing through the city's flowers seeped into Mary's mind, and as if some drowsy spell had been lifted, she knew inside her heart, that Roxanne's garden had crab trees and brambles, and they were hers, not Mary's.

She woke up to light peeking through the window. Her body was warm and fragrant; her face was cool and fresh as a morning flower. A breeze gently pushed through the old lace curtains; Mary remembered about Roxanne's screaming and Shirley's griddle whacking grief, and most of all Griffens sadness. She simple lay there for a minute feeling the strange garden of her own heart. Maybe that's why Arlene spent so much time outside.

The coolness of the morning whispered that there wasn't much she could do, not much she could do at all. She pushed herself to a sitting position, stockinged feet touching the cool floor, and her whole body stretched up to standing, arms reaching out as wide as the morning. Cool air entering her nose filled her lungs, and then that restless wind moved back up through her lips and out again into the morning, carrying a sigh. For the briefest of moments she wondered who is Mary Blu, anyway.

Without even wanting to put slippers on she padded into the bathroom, sat on the smooth cool toilet seat and released a torrent of vexation. She wiped herself, some thoughts brewing deep down inside. She washed her hands and face and brushed her teeth. On the way back to the bedroom the coiled braid caught her attention. While cars whirred by outside and steps grated to a rhythm that echoed off the apartment walls, she sat down and began caressing and sewing the braid into an ever widening circle.

She made it to work just in time. Instead of rushing back to the kitchen she had a brief mission to accomplish. First she went to the table of her friends. "Hi." She paused too excited to say anymore.

"Hello honey, my! That au naturel look suites you. You keep looking so good, you'll put me out of work."

Mary blushed and took a little gasp of air.

"Howdy mam."

Mary smiled at Tex and breathed a little easier.

"Good morning Mary Blu." Griffin squirmed trying not to stare at her too long.

Mary noticed that his eyes no longer searched her out. Of course they wouldn't after what she had done…she remembered his sadness last night, remembered it softly. Of course she knew that whatever had happened with tea and oranges and chicken soup was over now. Funny how she missed that.

That sense of having lost something beyond hope allowed her to go on. "You see there's this rug I'm making. I'm making it from rags. It's going real well, but I just need a few more, ah, you know rags. And I wonder if maybe each of you might have some old raggedy piece of clothes that you could give me, not much, but just something from each of you to finish up with."

The sound of a griddle being scraped stopped. "Hey doll, this is a restaurant not a Good Will Store. You gotta be kidding!"

Without waiting for a reply, Mary fled, almost tripping over a swiveling stool at the counter. Even after she disappeared behind the swinging door to the kitchen, it spun a couple of more times.

Mary's heart stopped thumping in her ears as she pushed a large tray into the puffing dish washing machine...so far so good. She had one more mission to accomplish yet today, and it would be the hardest, maybe the hardest thing that she ever done.

At 5 p.m. she rinsed down the sink. She heard the exact moment that the dish washing machine clicked off. It was time. That sound signaled the start of her dangerous enterprise. She pulled her hair net off; each movement was in slow motion. She processed from the kitchen through the restaurant where she picked up her tips, and out into the street. Each step, each face she passed on the sidewalk was a revelation. She couldn't think about what she was doing, and let the purpose of her feet and the coincidence of the afternoon carry her on. Today was a good day to die.

She walked past her apartment and around the corner stopping in front of a small white house with a porch that sagged towards the sidewalk with abandoned hope Up on that sorry porch an old sofa soaked by fall rains dared anybody to sit on it. Mary stepped up the sidewalk covered with red scrawling writing, "LIAR, LIAR PANTS ON FIRE...LIAR, LIAR MARY BLUES PANTS ARE ON FIRE." Mary stepped onto the spongy wood of the porch. The aluminum door with no screen in it swung half opened. She carefully opened it and tapped on the front door.

The house was dark as if it were a place in which no one dared turn on a light. She thought she heard little steps running back into the shadowy house. Mary stood there in front of the glassed windowed door as firmly planted as a tree. She smelled the moldy sofa and the dark fumes of a truck that had just passed by. There, a yellow light turned on in the living room piled with clothes and boxes. A woman moved towards the door startled as if woken from a dream. A dress covered with faded flowers hung forlornly on her thin body; she futilely attempted to straighten the mussed tresses of her hair. Right in front of the door she caught her own reflection mirrored in the glass. Her face automatically frowned as she straightened her dress out over her body. She opened the door barely an inch, peeking out.

Mary shifted a little from side to side. "Oh I'm so sorry to bother you, but I know a little girl named Roxanne and I think she lives here."

The woman stiffened as if she were waiting for calamitous news, but remained silent.

"I just wanted to make sure to say good bye to Roxanne. I know you're both going away. I think she's mad at me. I still want to say good bye; I promised. And saying goodbye is all I can do."

The woman's face relaxed and the door opened an inch further. "I don't know what gets into her sometimes. One minute it's Mary Blu this and Mary Blu that, and the next she's so mad at you slaming every door in the house. She's a good girl, but kind of wild. I suppose I haven't been much help since my husband died. Did she tell you about that?"

Mary's whole face melted in sympathy.

The sympathy must have been too much. The face behind the opening turned stony and the gap cautiously narrowed once again. "I'll tell Roxanne you called." The door closed.

Chapter 20

Mary Blu walked home in the solitary chill of evening. The sidewalks and the roads were clearing; most people in the city were already at the place they called home. Mary felt invisible, or at least something like invisible: she didn't care if people were looking at her now. A thin old man, with hair and beard dyed coal black carrying a brown paper bag from the liquor store looked up at her with shining eyes when he passed. No, she mustn't be invisible to other people, maybe she was just invisible to herself. Usually her eyes peeked out waiting to spot someone looking at her big and clumsy and fat and stupid self. Suddenly instead of the wide world, all she would be able to see was ridiculous image she called Mary Blu. But this time, when the black bearded man looked at her with his pirate eyes, she simply saw a black bearded man looking at her as he walked by...that's all. She kept walking into the evening's sights and smells and sounds.

Funny she should feel like this now. Her friend and

her boss were mad at her; Griffin was kind but probably disappointed. She really didn't know what Tex and Dannie thought about her, but they must see the mess she's made. How come she felt so good? Well, maybe not good...how come she simply felt. After all there wasn't much more to loose anymore.

She opened the door to her apartment, flicked the light on and saw this little place that was her home. She decided that tonight would be special treat. She'd make macaroni and cheese again, but this time, after it was all cooked up in the sauce pan, she'd scoop it out and put it into a little roasting pan. She had some left over broccoli which she could mix in. Then for the final and magic step...she would open a can of French fried onion rings and carefully place the rings on top of her mixture. She was so excited she could hardly stand it.

After slipping her invention into the oven; she took a long, hot shower, closing her eyes and letting the water rush against her face. She took a clean towel and buffed herself dry, all the while sniffing cheese and onion roasting. She never knew that food could be so much fun. Pulling on a clean Star Trek tee shirt and crisp dungarees, she walked back into the kitchen, opening a cupboard, and pulled out a bottle of wine. She poured out the last of the red liquid into a plastic glass.

That night she sat in the big second floor window, sipping wine, contentedly eating a new dish she called Mary Blu Supreme, and listening. Besides she knew now who to thank for the music that turned sparkling lights on throughout the city.

About 8:30 that night...the music stilled and the last of supper dishes carefully dried and put away, Mary heard an insistent banging coming from the back of the house. First she tried to settle down to do some more sewing on her rug. The banging continued; dogs were starting to bark. She got up from the floor and stepped out on the back landing to reconnoiter. There in the murky glow of the street light, she saw Roxanne banging a trash can with a stick almost as big as she was.

Even though Mary could see her breath in the night air, she sat down on the steps. Roxanne stopped her banging just long enough to peak up sideways to make sure Mary was listening. Mary was.

Roxanne started banging again, but before long she glanced up at Mary for the briefest of instants. Then she turned away; her banging got louder. She glanced up again, and again her banging got louder, but this time she fastened her gaze on Mary just a little longer...her banging started softening. Roxanne looked up again, eyes now resting on Mary...silence in the alley...Roxanne was watching Mary Blu, maybe even listening.

That was what Mary was waiting for. "Hey Roxanne, how about some coolaid?"

Roxanne tightened in a moment of futile resistance and then ran up the stairs so fast that she was standing next to her friend even before Mary had pulled herself up to a standing position. Mary noticed something pink and faded tied around Roxanne's waist.

They walked into the kitchen that was still warm, smelling of roasted Mary Blu Supreme. While Mary opened the refrigerator and poured coolaid, Roxanne plopped down right next to the rug. "But Mary, who's gonna help you finish the rug if I go?"

Mary walked into the living room slowly, not with caution, there was too much grace of movement for that. She handed Roxanne her coolaid and sat down on the floor too. The coiling rug lay between them. "Roxanne Crabtree somethings a person needs to do by herself. I guess finishing this rug is one of those things for me."

Clearly that wasn't what Roxanne wanted to hear. Her whole body balled up against the floor; her face looked down and squished so tight it almost disappeared into a bitter frown. The two sat there on each side of the rug.

Finally when Mary was sure that she wasn't frightened of Roxanne any more, she stood up and silently walked over and settled herself down next to her friend. She didn't say anything; she just sat there. By some means of mysterious and accidental sympathy her breath began going in and out with the rhythm of Roxanne's breathing. There…now they were breathing together. Neither was following the other, they were simply breathing in sympathy, speeding up, slowing down creating a pattern together. Roxanne was slowly unfolding, and Mary was amazed that she could feel so much for a person without trying to save her.

As natural and unselfconscious as a tide moving in, Mary began talking. "Roxanne, you're my first friend. I've loved people before like my sister, Arlene, and a couple of people that I worked with, but we weren't friends, because I always thought I was just too stupid. So if anything scary happened to them, I thought I was supposed to fix it. I had to make things better for them, I had too; and all the time I was running around like crazy."

She settled into a quiet sitting position. "One day I realized that they didn't want what I wanted for them. Arlene wanted to get married and go to Alaska, and those two people I worked with, it was even more confusing... they wanted things that hurt me. It was so hard for me to see that we were separate, because I never wanted to be separate and all alone. I don't know if this makes any sense to you Roxanne Crabtree, because it's just starting to make sense to me."

Mary stopped talking for a moment. She noticed that Roxanne's eyes were open.

After a little breathing together, Mary started again. "You're my first friend Roxanne because I know we are separate. You have your own mother and your own life. You learn things fast, and I'm a little slower. You know how to figure out the difference between right and left without even thinking, and for me I need to learn how to find which side is which. I know all about using a dish washer, and you don't yet. I know what it's like to be an older woman and see some of the things I was most afraid of, happen. I know what it is like not to live with anybody. When I was walking home from your house, I knew that for me it was finally all right to be alone. That's why right now I can be your friend."

Mary paused again, as if she were listening to herself and wanted to make sure that she was really understanding what she was saying. "I can't take you away from your mother, I can't stop you from going to Milwaukee. I don't even know if it's good or bad that you're going there. I do know, and I really know this Roxanne, that I feel real sad that you're going away, and I'll do everything I know how, to keep being your friend. I'll write letters and even get a phone. And Roxanne, I'll always know that you are my first friend. You can always know, no matter if things get really bad, that there is one person who is proud to be your friend."

"I'm really your first friend Mary, your very first friend?" Roxanne was sitting straight now as if she were about to receive a prize.

Mary smiled. "A few months back, I left my home and my job and everything I knew. I was so frightened, I couldn't even think about being frightened; I just kind of got all sleepy. Right on my last day at the Rainbow, that's where I used to work; this woman named Ariadne who was even older than me, talked to me and gave me the yellow scarf that you see on the sofa."

Mary rose to standing and picked up that scarf. As she approached Roxanne, it fluttered behind her like a brilliant yellow flag. So much beauty dazzled Roxanne's eyes; Mary knelt right in front of her in the very center of the growing, Technicolor circle, and tied that scarf around Roxanne's neck. "Now Ariadne told me that sometimes things get real hard and painful, and when you find that there's nothing else you can do about it, it's time to relax and let go all the while knowing that you are doing the best you can…and that's enough."

Mary looked into Roxanne's eyes and neither looked away. "This scarf is a reminder of that and of me. And maybe someday you'll find someone who needs this scarf as much as I did and you do, and by that time maybe you'll remember so well how wonderful you are and how good a friend you are, that you can give it away too."

Tears were dribbling out of Roxanne's eyes. She was making little sniffling sounds and wiping her nose with her right wrist. "I have something for you too Mary." She dropped her head for a moment and started to untie a raggedy pink piece of cloth tied around her waist. "This is for your rug, you know because there's clothes from your mom and dad and Arlene, and I thought maybe you might like something from me too." She held the pink cloth out without looking up, standing there as if waiting for something terrible to happen.

"Oh Roxanne, pink, that'll be just beautiful. Al I have left is just some brown material from my mother's old house dress. Towards the end of her life she only wore dark, muddy colors. And then I have this stained white shirt from my father. This pink mixed in will make those memories beautiful. It would even cheer them up a little."

Roxanne's eyes held Mary's gaze. "That's a dress my daddy gave me before he caught that grapefruit sickness. I'm too big for it now." A smile flickered hesitantly on Roxanne's facea as if she wasn't quite sure if the coast was clear. Finally the smile won out. "Can we make strips now Mary, please. I can help you braid a little. I promise I'll leave the last part for you."

In a flash, they were both sitting down. First Mary cut some strips of pink, and then Roxanne cut up that brown dress and those shirts. Mary placed the pink strip between the brown and white. Roxanne began braiding with her special flair. For a moment there weren't goodbyes or even time; they were simply braiding.

But even forever ends because without an ending; nothing new could start with out mystery. Mary noticed it first. She could felt soreness in her lower back, a vague feeling of unease. She tried shifting her position, but the soreness was still there. Her whole large body began fidgeting. The old Mary Blu would have tried to forget about that feeling and keep sitting with Roxanne, but after all the amazing adventures of the past few months, she actually knew what she needed to do without even thinking about it. She simply stood up.

Roxanne's hands were starting to slow up, that stony look on her face starting to harden.

Mary knew forever was ending.

Roxanne watched Mary suspiciously and something more, maybe even curiosity. She stood up, too.

Mary suddenly looked alarmed.

Roxanne tilted her head to the side, bewildered at Mary's expression.

Suddenly Mary's mouth dropped open… "Roxanne, how am I going to get a hold of you? I don't know you're new address or your phone number even. I don't want to loose you completely."

They stood absolutely still, wide open eyes staring back and forth, shocked and stumped by the problem. After all Roxanne was leaving tomorrow morning, and all the good intentions in the world couldn't prevent them from being torn apart forever. Even a goodbye didn't take the pain of that thought away.

Mary who had longer experience in losing, surfaced first. "Roxanne maybe you could ask your mother. Maybe she has the address or phone number of her boyfriend." They looked back and forth at each other, but the fear was still there. Mary tried again. "I'll give you my address and when you get there you can write me."

Even though Mary looked pretty content with that idea, Roxanne didn't seem reassured. "I never wrote a letter before. I'd need all kinds of stuff, like an envelope and a stamp and paper and someplace to mail it at." Her voice trailed off to a whine.

Mary decided to try again. "Well, I know your last name, and I'll call information."

Roxanne was banging her fist on her leg now. "MARY, don't you see that the phone would be in that dumb guy's name, and mom just calls him Ted?"

For a moment Mary's whole bodied throbbed with desperate agitation.

"Don't be stupid Mary. What are we going to do?"

That's when Mary noticed something bouncing around inside herself again. She became so curious about it, that she forgot to be so desperate and wobbly; her whole body settled into introspection. Maybe it was the influence of the Star Trek tee shirt, but she was exploring the final frontier. She looked up at Roxanne with the sobriety of a Star Trek captain, her body settling into the serenity of someone used to facing death. She put her hand on Roxanne's tight little shoulder. "Roxanne Crabtree, I'll give you my address and try my best to get a hold of you, I promise. I won't forget you, just like the way your dress is part of my rug. But I want you to try too to get ahold of me. I want you to try your best to reach me."

Roxanne was thrashing now. "MARY, you're supposed to do something!"

Mary was silent, her head hardly wobbled at all.

Roxanne popped up from the floor, her fists pounding the air. She ran from the apartment.

Mary said goodbye to the slamming door.

Chapter 21

Mary was almost late for work that next morning. She was just putting some last stitches on the rug; that brown, pink and white braid was absolutely perfect. Stepping through the door of Surely's she felt a gust of smoky, bacon sizzling air. Yes...excitement was bouncing around inside her. One minute she felt sick to her stomach and the next she noticed how bright and alive Surely's seemed. She looked over at the table of her friends. Tex was holding what looked like a worn, red plaid shirt. In front of Mr. Dannie sat a shiny pile of a scarlet red shirt. Griffin was holding a pair of old blue jeans, as pale and blue as a spring morning.

Hardly embarrassed at all she simply said, "Thanks," and took the bundles.

She heard a voice behind. "Hey doll get over here!"

Mary did.

"Take it, just take!" Shirley pushed a pile of old black velvet across the far from spotless counter.

Mary squeezed out a thank you.

"You gotta be kidding."

With the four bundles of cloth in her hands, she walked back to the kitchen with something like happiness bouncing around inside. Having an inside wasn't so bad after all. It left room for lots of different feelings. Somehow with an inside...well, it just can't be explained by words. She shook her head. The outside wasn't so scary; it was simple like just what is happening.. even inside was just what is happening. She stared off in space, or was it staring inside. Funny how it gets all mixed up, but not in a bad way exactly.

She did dishes that day with a kind of simple grace that would have even broken the heart of a disappointed dance teacher. Sometimes when a tray of dishes had been placed in the machine, and it clicked on suddenly, water inside the mysterious belly starting to spray; she remembered about Roxanne and felt sad, a deep but simple pain that ran a course of its own. Funny when she actually listened to the bouncing around inside, it wasn't so terrible. All she had to do was know that she was trying her best and then let go, no matter what was going on.

That afternoon after pulling her damp hair net off, she picked up her four piles of cloth. What wonderful braids those colors would make. She could mix the reds and blacks and plaids blues in amazing combinations that she knew would be just perfect for her rug.

She stepped through the swinging door and grabbed her tips; Shirley had just puffed out a cloud of smoke and was adding numbers on a greasy sheet of paper. She looked up for a moment…a strange look, not angry or sad, or even tender. It was more like surprise. And then she buried herself in that sheet full of figures and took a long heavy drag from her cigarette and forgot to say, "You gotta be kidding."

It was only when Mary stepped out the door to go home, that her newly discovered insides clenched. Roxanne would already be gone. There would be no one waiting for her, excited and squirmy; there would be no one to make coolaid for…so this was what it was like to be sad. Mary walked slowing feeling her stomach wrench and then slowly loosen…sad. Rushing people passed her. When she walked by the liquor store, she noticed the familiar old man with dyed hair and pirate eyes standing in front of the door asking for spare change. Mary suddenly knew that that man had insides too. She searched through her dungarees and found a quarter. She placed it in his hand just to let him know that she knew he was there.

She kept walking; she stood in front of the big old house that held her apartment. There written at least a hundred times in dark blue was the name "Ted Muellenbeck, Ted Muellenbeck, Ted Muellenbeck."

Chapter 22

That fall Mary got her very first telephone. At first she didn't get many calls except from people trying to sell newspapers and magazines and condominiums in Florida. Patiently she would listen to their pleas; then she would say that she didn't want to buy whatever they were selling. Finally she would say, "Well I sure hope things work out for you; life can be pretty hard." Sometimes the person on the other end of the line would hang up before she finished talking. Sometimes the person on the other end of the line took her good bye as a sign of interest and would hopefully repeat their spiel. A woman from Waseka selling cable television subscriptions burst into tears and then thanked Mary.

And yes, she found Ted Muellenbeck's number in the Milwaukee phone book, and every other Friday evening she called Roxanne. The two didn't talk long, after all Mary didn't have much money, but somehow the very regularity of those calls made the days and the weeks wind in some, if not meaning, at least moments of connection.

And then people started calling. First Tex, and then Dannie, and then Shirley. One night in October, when the yellow and red leaves were a damp muddy memory, the phone rang. "Hi Mary Blue. This is Griffin."

"Oh, ah Griffin." Mary took in a deep breath and held it while her eyes got bigger and bigger.

"I don't mean to bother you, but Tex was saying that...that friend of yours, you know the little girl, lives in Milwaukee. Just the other day I was thinking that I've never really been to Milwaukee, and it might be an interesting place to visit, and besides I've got a car now. It's kind of old but…" As Griffin spoke his voice was becoming more and more tentative until it disappeared all together.

Something was bouncing around so rapidly inside Mary that she could hardly breathe, but she knew she needed to say something. "I'm so glad you called Griffin. You're going to Milwaukee?"

That was enough to hearten Griffin. "Well, I was wondering if you want to come with me. I know you must have all kinds of people who want to be with you."

"Ummmmm."

"We could leave real early in the morning, and we could stop at Roxanne's, and even be back by night time." His voice stopped.

Whatever was inside Mary was bouncing around so fast that she didn't have space to be embarrassed. "Griffin... yes, for sure."

That evening she had planned to finish her rug, but

after talking with Griffin, she was too excited to thing about finishing anything for a while. She sat in the very center of her rug, the colors of people in her life weaving in and out and making patterns in strange and beautiful ways. The pink, the flashy turquoise, the pale blue, the muddy brown and even the angry black all spun out all around her, experiences running through her until for a moment, she, the very large and clumsy, Mary Blue, flickered, and for an instant, disappeared.

Then, matter of factly, she bent over and touched the loose and unfinished end of braid peaking out at the edge of the circle. Now Mary may not have always thought in clear why's and wherefore's, but sitting in that very center, color rippling out through her, she knew that she would keep that loose end unfinished. Who knows what new people and colors were going to happen along.

THE END